All for One

Ancient Middle Eastern Sword Cocktail Toothpicks

Richard Baran

Mouse Gate™.
1103 Middlecreek
Friendswood, Texas 77546
281-992-3131 TEL
www.mousegate.com

Copyright © 2019 by: Richard Baran
Edited by: William R. "Will" Barshop
Copy Editors, Carol Fredrickson, Julie Laren,
Special Editing and Formatting: William B. Symank
All rights reserved

ISBN: 978-1-59095-356-3
UPC: 6-43977-43568-2

Printed in the United States of America with simultaneous printings in Australia, Canada, and United Kingdom.

FIRST EDITION
1   2   3   4   5   6   7   8   9   10

Dedication:

C.A.: Playground swings, growing old together
and love forever. R.T.

To: Will, Gracie, Elsa Jane and Rile

About the Book

William *Worm* Bell Sizemore, Robert *Shakers* Allen, Jr., Ricky *Chief* Lightfoot and Farah *Royal* Smolinksi are eighth grade friends; with Farah the lone girl. They call themselves the Four Musketeers and have a one for all and all for one bond. According to Will's grandfather, a crusty old Navy veteran: "You four are thicker than a band of thieves."

It was Will's grandfather and an early spring thunder storm complete with tornado warnings that changed the four lives forever. Will's grandfather had presented his grandson with four miniature scimitars. The ancient Middle Eastern swords resembled gold cocktail toothpicks. They were more than that. The scimitars were said to be magical, each possessing one wish for the person who held it.

Robert Allen, Jr. was called **Shakers** by his other Musketeers because his birth was the product of an inter-racial marriage. His mother Puerto Rican and his father of Scandinavian heritage. Both were college professors. Both were killed in a drive-by shooting; mistaken targets.

Ricky Lightfoot, the most cantankerous and opinionated of the four, was an Ojibwa Indian, a Lake Superior Chippewa of the Lac du Flambeau band. He was called **Chief** because, according to him: "You palefaces speak with forked tongue and I don't trust a one of you." Then, before his three friends could verbally attack him, he would come up with his hasty declaimer stating: "**Shakers**, you and **Royal** ain't ever gonna be pale. As for you, **Worm**, you ain't ever gonna be red, black or brown from sitting under a reading lamp all day and night. I can trust you."

Farah *Royal* Smolinksi's mother was from the Middle East; presumably, Iran where it was rumored that a late female relative of hers had been married to the Shah of Iran. Therefore, according to her three male friends, she had descended from a Queen or some type of royalty. It stood to reason in the minds of *Worm, Shakers* and *Chief* that she should have a name that connotated regal status. *Queenie* didn't work, but *Royal* did. Besides, she was the smartest of the group sporting an A+ average and a phenomenal athlete; at five feet nine, a basketball player. Brains and basketball prowess weren't her only assets. She was beautiful and each of her three friends had a silent crush on her. She had a silent crush on *Worm*.

Part I

Chapter 1

William Bell Sizemore, *Will* or *Worm* to his friends, had few dislikes as he was about to enter year two of his teen years. Besides hating lima beans; "They taste like that lumpy paste we used in kindergarten," he would utter to the three other family members seated at the large, ornate oak kitchen table where all the Sizemore meals were eaten; all with a muted television.

Will's other dislike was being labeled a *Book Worm* by his father who loved lima beans and insisted his son would also love them.

Will knew better than to give expanded, detailed complaints about a lima bean, omitting facial distortions knowing those would ignite a wrath from his father. His complaining would have no effect on one of many Sizemore family idiosyncrasies pertaining to food and its consumption. There were few rules pertaining to eating, those rules centered on being a member of the Sizemore Family Clean Plate Club or, as Will's grandfather would so succinctly remind him, "My parents and grandparents lived through the Great Depression. They didn't have the luxury to waste food." The "CPC Rule" (Clean Plate Club as enacted by Will's grandfather and enforced by his father) was that no one left the table until all evidence of food on one's plate had been removed. Will knew he would lose the stare down between himself and the disgusting portion of green legumes leering up at him. He always did. Yet, he never stopped trying. That was Will Sizemore summed up in one word; Determined.

Will's passion in life, besides hanging out with his three best friends, was reading. It was his grandfather who hooked him on the printed word. Will respected the old man who looked anything but old. His grandfather looked like he should have been doing television commercials for health clubs. He still sported a crewcut from his youth, the color now silver setting off a stern face that was showing a crazy quilt of lines shooting out from eyes that offset the serious face. His grandfather had dumped a worn, faded book into Will's lap one evening as he was seated Indian style on the worn living room carpet, a large floral design somehow having escaped the battering of foot traffic over the years. He was in front of the outdated television watching a snowy, faded color rerun of a movie scene that resembled chariot races in a Roman coliseum. "I saw your last report card," his grandfather said with a frown, his face reflecting his displeasure. "Looks like you never opened any of your books." The old man paused, continued to frown then added with a touch of sarcasm, "You do know how to read, don't you?"

Will knew better than to answer with a smirk the way he did with some of his teachers at Thorpe School, but never his favorite teacher, Mr. Toll who taught history and also doubled as an Assistant Principal and Guidance Counselor. "I know how to read, Grandpa," he replied respectfully.

"I thought you did," his grandfather said. "For awhile I was concerned that you liked that school of yours so much that you wanted to spend a couple of happy years in each grade."

Will smiled at his grandfather. "Oh, Grandpa, you're too much."

"Don't tell me something I already know," the old man said, his close cropped silver-grey crew cut making him look like a veteran who had stormed ashore during one too many wars of years gone by. He was, however, a veteran, a Navy one. His specialty had him working on the hydraulic systems of aircraft. In Navy jargon, he was an Airedale; a Bubble Chaser. His service started at the tail end of the Korean Conflict and ended with the heating up of an ongoing conflict in Viet Nam after the French got their lunch handed to them by who they thought were an undermanned, underequipped rag tag bunch of Asian peasants. "This country of ours never could stay out of a war," he explained to Will. He nodded at the hard cover book that had slid off Will's lap and was face down on the carpet. "Is that how you treat a gift from your grandfather?"

Will gave him a puzzled look.

"I don't want to confuse you," his grandfather said, his sarcastic mode gaining the momentum that Will both loved and hated, sometimes even feared. He continued to nod at the book with the faded grey cloth cover and worn corners. "But that's no way to treat a book. Books are the greatest gift any man can receive." He paused, pursed his lips and continued: "That is, any man with half a functioning brain would recognize that fact of life." He paused again and stared at his grandson, a twinkle in his eye. "You do have more than half a brain, don't you Will?"

Will politely ignored his grandfather's last remark and addressed the one before it. "You mean a woman can't get a book for a gift," said Will, knowing that this was an opportunity when he could joke with his grandfather. "You're not being politically correct, Grandpa." A respectful smiled followed.

"You'll think differently about what's correct and what's not correct when I give you a crack across your prat," his grandfather said.

Will gave him a questioning look.

"Your butt, Dumbkopf," his grandfather said, the slight trace of a German accent visible. "Pratfall is a saying from old vaudeville shows where one on the comics would end up taking a hard fall on his behind." His grandfather shook his head from side to side several times. "You and your generations don't know beans about anything," he stated and then continued on with a question that he would answer. "And, do you know why? It's because you have your faces glued up against the screens of those cell phones of yours. None of you know how to talk to one another and darn few of you, if any, know how to read."

Will smiled and reached for the book with his near hand. He held it up. "Don't worry, Grandpa, I'll read it."

"I know you will," his grandfather said and then paused. "And, so does your butt."

*****

Will never forgot that evening when his grandfather introduced him to an exciting new world. His addiction to his new cell phone that he had pleaded with his father to get seemed to vanish when he was introduced to Todd Moran. Todd, as Will discovered thanks to one of the last official uses of his cell phone and the internet, was a character in an adventure story created by Howard Pease. Actually, Pease had written a series of adventure stories with his main character, not too much older than Will, running away from home and joining the Merchant Marines. Will's grandfather had read the story when he was the same age as his grandson. Todd Moran, the young adventurer, had found himself onboard one tramp steamer after another heading all over the Seven Seas eventually ending up in foreboding, unheard of locales that raised the hair on Will's arms as he soaked up every word. The book his grandfather had so unceremoniously given him two years ago, The Black Tanker, exploded Will's hunger to learn more about what existed beyond the constraints of Will's northwest side Chicago neighborhood. His new passion for reading quickly led him, to his grandfather's delight, to making the Honor Roll and being accepted into Lane Tech for high school.

Howard Pease stayed Will's favorite author as his quest to read everything he could get his hands on grew. He harvested words; all words, especially Pease's. At times, he would read the Dictionary. Academic disciplines began to both intrigue and interest him almost as much as Pease's specialties about being a crewman on board the dirtiest most rusted hulks at sea; the more mysterious, almost evil looking the cargo ship, the better. The first two and a half pages of the book his grandfather had unceremoniously dumped in his lap were all it took to capture Will's imagination forever and turn him into who his father referred to as, "My son, the Bookworm."

Will remembered his grandfather standing in front of the television and not realizing that a hand had gone behind a back to turn the set off. There had been the almost gentle warning: "I want you to read for ten minutes every night before you go to bed. No cell phone stuff. No texting. No Selfies. No Sexting." His grandfather had grinned as Will blushed trying to figure out how anyone so old would know about the latest cell phone craze among his peers. Then his grandfather had added. "Who in the heck would want to see a skinny runt like you prancing around in his underwear?" He gave a shrug. "Well, at least you don't look like a shaggy dog like so many of your friends," His grandfather continued. "Too bad those donkeys don't know what a comb is or where the nearest barber shop is located."

*****

Early in Will's life, about the time he was tasting kindergarten paste, his mother had died. To this day he didn't know why. He never accepted the fact that he was a kid in school that didn't have a mother. All the kids at Thorpe School had mothers waiting for them at home except one of his friends, Robert Allen, Jr. who lived with his Puerto Rican grandmother. Both of Robert's parents had died, accidentally shot and killed. That's what the police and the news had stated and their statements were true.

Will also lived with his grandmother as well as his dad and grandfather.

Will's dad never remarried although a parade of women, none looking like his mother, came and went, his dad not appearing to seek any form of approval from his son for his choice in female companionship and Will not offering any. Then the parade seemed to stop, Will not noticing at first. What he did notice was his father becoming very quiet. So quiet that he even stopped insisting that his son should eat lima beans. When that new freedom in eating habits began to roll on into several weeks Will started getting nervous and he mentioned his feelings to his grandfather

"Why is my father so quiet lately, Grandpa?" asked Will trying to suppress a growing sense of fear that might have him end up like his friend, Robert Allen, Jr. who lived with a solitary grandmother. "And, Grandpa it will be almost a month since we've had lima beans appear on our kitchen table."

Will, unlike Robert Allen, Jr. had both of his grandparents living with him along with his father in their Cape Cod style house a few short blocks from Addison and Austin and Wright Junior College.

"Will," his grandfather started out after putting his arm around his shoulder, "your dad appears to be coming to grips with his new life."

"One without Mom?" he asked.

His grandfather nodded and gave Will's shoulder a gentle squeeze. No more words were said. No more words were necessary.

Will shared the incident with his friend, Robert Allen, Jr. who was known as *Shakers*. Robert had lost both of his parents, both innocent victims in a senseless drive-by shooting in Hyde Park where they had worked. Will had heard the story when he and Robert first met, before the name, *Shakers* became an identity. Will had never felt numb before, but he never forgot how Robert Allen, Jr. rambled on about his mother and father, the once college professors at what Will thought he heard was the University of Chicago. The facts and muddled details had stayed buried in the muddy grave of Robert's mind. The why's, where's and how-comes of the tragedy appearing in the forms of choked sobs from his grandmother. His mother and father had been on their way to their favorite little side street bistro to celebrate their both getting tenure in their respective departments. Then a drug deal went south and Robert's parents were on their way in another direction, this one leading them into the hereafter. Robert soon found himself living with his *Gramma* River, as he called her, Rios her Puerto Rican name. He had gone from the south side of Chicago to the far northwest side to live on the first floor of a two-flat owned by her in a neighborhood that had barely enough Puerto Ricans to fill the back seat of one cab in San Juan. Robert soon acquired the creative nickname, *Shakers* from three of his new classmates at Thorpe School; Will Sizemore,

Ricky Lightfoot and Farah Smolinki. *Shakers* was short for salt and pepper shakers, symbolic of the black and white that Robert's mother, a stunning, black skinned Puerto Rican and his father, a gangly bean pole of a man of Scandinavian heritage, were an interracial couple.

Will, Robert, Rickey and Farah became inseparable, their bond one of the Musketeers— "one for all and all for one." With their unique senses of humor, they added to the pledge by saying, "and I go first."

The four had bonded on first sight and seemed glued together at the hips when they were in grammar school. None of their other classmates could figure out why this unlikely quartet could be such close friends. They were as different as different could be. Somehow the three were always there when one of them was in need. As Will had said to the others early on in their friendship: "We're like a team of horses pulling a chariot or a stagecoach," he had said, then pausing to think, to disarm his three critics. "I mean a stagecoach has more horses, but they all work together."

Rickey and Farah also had their creative nicknames, wearing them with pride. Ricky Lightfoot was, as he preferred to call himself, *Chief*; his family were members of the Lake Superior Chippewa from the Lac du Flambeau band of Ojibwa. The U.S. Mint might have chosen Ricky's profile for the nickel; minus, of course, his youthful age and the feather. There wasn't one hanging from his long jet-black hair. "My people were in this country long before you pale faces got here," he would state to his three friends, a convoluted pride beaming from him. Then he'd catch himself, apologize to Robert and say, "Sorry, Shakers, you ain't ever gonna be pale like those other two." He would nod at Will and Farah. "You're dark enough to be one of my people but your darkness came from too many blends of salt and pepper coming together on that Caribbean island of yours."

"Boring," Farah Smolinski would cry out after hearing Ricky's explanation on ethnic differences. Farah was the lone girl in the quartet. She was tall for her age, almost five feet nine, and as dark skinned as Ricky and Robert. Farah had large, piercing hypnotic dark eyes and was rumored to have come from Middle Eastern royalty, a one-too-many time removed relative on her mother's side that had a title of, Shah for one of its male members. Her father, Walter Smolinski, a truck driver for a meat packing company off of Randolph Street in Chicago's market area, always gave the impression he wasn't interested in his wife's supposed royal blood line stating, "Ain't nothin' that comes out of the dessert except oil, Arabs and camel *gufna*."

Farah's three friends tended to agree with her father's Polish description of camel excrement and always found creative ways to remind her.

That didn't deter Farah. She was convinced of her royalty.

"Yeah, right," replied Will after hearing Farah boast of her regal ancestry yet again. "Whadda ya want us to do, bow down and call you Queenie?"

"Queen," would be sufficient," she would state. "It has a nice sound of royal formality to it." Then she would brace herself for a chorus of cat calls from her three friends; the call followed by the three guys taking out their cell phones and turning the flashlight portions on and putting her in the spotlight. She loved the verbal hazing and basking in their light beams.

Farah Smolinski also loved athletics. She was a gifted athlete. Being tall meant she was perceived as a basketball player; either that or a fashion model. She could have been both, but she loved sports and basketball was her passion. Farah wasn't a good basketball player. She was a great one. Every high school coach in Chicago wanted her on their team. Private school coaches recruited her. They all but drooled over her talents. Her friends were especially in awe of her prowess on the hard court. According to Will, Ricky and Robert, "You could be playing for the Bulls. None of them guys getting millions could guard you. Not even Michael Jordan in his day." He paused and looked at Ricky and Robert for agreement knowing that the three of them were too young to appreciate what Michael Jordan could do with a basketball when he played. Getting it, he said, "That Le Braun James guy from Cleveland couldn't guard you."

Farah loved the attention of being compared to great professional basketball players, male and female. But, her love of basketball had nothing to do with the nickname that evolved for her. *Royal* soon shoved aside Queenie and Queen.

*****

Worm, Shaker, Royal and Chief were as united like the chariot drawn by the team of four horses that Will had seen on a television movie. They were closer than any band of brothers or, as they quickly adjusted their status to, Inseparable Siblings. It was Worm's grandfather who often remarked, "You kids are thicker than thieves."

Worm and the others didn't grasp the analogy at first. Then Will's grandfather dropped another worn, hard cover book alongside of his dinner plate one night; this dinner minus any resemblance of lima beans which made Will happy along with his stomach.

"I think you'll like this story," Will's grandfather said as he refilled his dark blue coffee mug with the etching of a golden anchor and U.S.N. embossed on both sides. "Maybe you won't give me that dumb look when I say that you and your friends are closer than a bunch of thieves."

Will turned the book in front of him so that the title on the cover was right side up. He gave a glance at his grandfather and then looked at the title again. "This is a cartoon book for kids, Grandpa. What gives?"

"Cartoon," his grandfather repeated softly. "I think not, Will. Let me know what you think after you've read some of it." He paused, his coffee cup to his lips and his eyes giving a dancing smile over the rim. "Surely I've told you enough times about never judging a book by its cover."

"Grandpa," said Will, a curiosity in his voice he couldn't conceal. "You never told me anything like that. All you ever told me is that you wanted to read for at least ten minutes every night before I go to bed. And I've done that. I've done it so much that my dad gets mad at me for staying up late instead of getting some sleep."

His grandfather took a sip of coffee, his eyes still dancing. "Well, then, read about Sinbad the Sailor; read about Ali Baba and the Forty Thieves and read about Arabian nights and magic lamps and flying carpets. Then we'll talk."

Chapter 2
Scimitars

Will took his new book about the Arabian nights up to his tiny bedroom that his father had built for him in the attic. This was his sanctuary and afforded him a sense of privacy even though limited. Limitations were set by his grandmother. She was constantly in and out of his room for any number of reasons ranging from cleaning to dropping off a basket of his clothes that needed folding after she had done the weekly wash which was always on a Monday. She never made an appearance at bed time. That was reserved for his father who would always trek up the stairs to the attic to have a short chat with his son, the chat always ending with: "Sleep tight and say a little prayer for your mother."

*****

That night, Will didn't sleep tight. He didn't sleep at all. He had tried. Tossing and turning was all he got for his efforts and the light on his night stand stayed glowing until the sun peered through his bedroom window. The light was one of his few possessions that he cared about. There was a small ship's wheel made of wood attached to a tarnished and scratched brass base. Across the yellow tinged shade were a series of ship silhouettes in black, all of old sailing ships. He loved the light and believed that Todd Moran surely had one in his bedroom before he followed the call of the Seven Seas.

Now, with the sun's help and his eyes heavy and the lids coated by a visit from the Sandman, Will reached for the latest book his grandfather had given him. Instead of opening and reading it earlier he had laid it on his stomach. Arabian nights weren't on his mind. His grandfather had shaken him up earlier that evening in the kitchen by placing what looked like by four pieces of plastic in his hand just before he had gone up the stairs to his attic bedroom. At first glance, the plastic pieces resembled fancy tooth picks. "Now that I'm sure you know how to read and have some resemblance of a brain because of your Honor Roll status," his grandfather had said to him from his customary seat at the head of the kitchen table, "I think you can handle these." He dropped the four-silver colored plastic looking tooth picks unceremoniously in his grandson's hand.

Will's face asked all the questions that needed to be asked and his grandfather answered each one in detail; too much detail for Will.

"Do you know what you have in your hand?" his grandfather had asked.

Will's reply was short and logical to him. "Fancy plastic toothpicks, Grandpa," he replied politely. "Kind of like the ones that are in the cabinet where my father keeps his liquor."

"Yeah, they kind of look like them don't they," his grandfather had said. "Look closer."

Will looked and looked some more before glancing at his grandfather. He shook his head back and forth several times.

"Look some more."

Will did having no idea what he was looking for. Then it hit him. The ends of the toothpicks were not pointed. "Grandpa," he said looking up. "These toothpicks you gave me are shaped like those big swords I've seen those Arab looking guys fighting with in a couple of movies and in some magazine pictures."

"Scimitars," his grandfather said.

"Yeah, big curved things with wide blades," said Will sounding excited. "They look like they weigh a ton." Will continued. "Pretty sharp too, I bet."

His grandfather nodded and his eyes seem to darken. "Sharp is an astute observation, Will," he said to his grandson. "You might also add, lethal."

"Lethal," Will said, repeating the word, his insides beginning to churn. "I guess they would be," he said his excitement cautiously growing along with his curiosity. "All of those guys I've seen swinging those things in the movies have muscles on their muscles, and those swords look like they're razor sharp."

"Razor sharp is another good way to describe them," his grandfather said with a smile. "Don't worry, Mister Book Worm," he said, "these miniature versions aren't lethal." He stopped and looked seriously at his grandson, more seriously than he had in his life. "They can be if you don't listen to what I have to say and treat them right."

"Really," gushed Will feeling the churning increasing. He glanced down to the palm of his right hand where his tiny scimitars sat glistening in the light from the kitchen's ceiling fixture, one of the three frosted bulbs burned out. "Grandpa," stated Will looking at his grandfather, "these things aren't plastic." He paused to take another look at the four items in his hand. "They look like they're made out of steel." He glanced at his grandfather. "They feel like it too."

"Very observant," said his grandfather looking very seriously at Will. "Be careful," he said softly. "Those things are as sharp as the razors you described." There was his customary pause before what Will knew was a warning about to come his way.

Will reached down with his left forefinger and touched the point of one of the blades. "Ouch," he said pulling back his finger. A tiny drop of blood emerged.

"I told you to be careful," his grandfather said. He reached into his shirt pocket and pulled out a tiny sheet of Kleenex from a cellophane packet and handed it to his grandson. "Looks like you're one of those guys who have to learn the hard way," he said.

Will took the tissue and placed it over his finger. He stood watching the crimson spot grow on the Kleenex and looking at the tiny swords in his palm at the same time. He focused his attention on the scimitars studying each and formulating his next question. "Why did you give me these?" he asked politely. "And, four of them?"

His grandfather smiled. "One for you and one each for those three other thieves you run around with." He laughed. "Tell them they're from me and that I just wanted to add a little excitement into their lives by introducing them to the Arabian Nights. You kids think that the whole world is the intersection of Addison and Austin," he said, his kind eyes smiling at Will. "Just be sure you warn them about how sharp they are. I don't want any irate parents or a Puerto Rican grandmother coming over here and taking me to court because I endangered a loved one's life." He gave a shrug and said, "I can't afford a liability law suit on my Social Security check."

"Grandpa, you are definitely too much."

"Again, you're telling me something I already know," his grandfather said way to serious. He stared at Will for what seemed like an eternity and said, "I'm warning you and you can warn your friends." He paused. "These so-called toothpicks looking things possess special powers."

Will almost jumped out of his skin. "Special powers?" he repeated. It took him a full minute to catch his breath before he asked, "Grandpa, are you telling me these things are magical?"

His grandfather nodded. "More than magical," he said.

"But, Grandpa…."

Will didn't get a chance to finish.

"They could save a life someday," his grandfather said. "Your life specifically," he continued and then nodding at the worn book he had dropped on the table earlier. "If you plan on giving these to your three friends like I intended for you to do, explain to them in detail the cautions I'm about to give you." He hesitated then continued. "I want you to listen very carefully to what I'm going to tell you. Then, when you give these to your friends, do not change one word, one letter, of my warnings." He paused again appearing to weigh each word he conveyed. "Any change could take away the magic. Any change could be dangerous. Any change might even be fatal."

The churning inside of Will suddenly stopped and he felt his body turn rigid; a chill going through him. It was as if he had been unceremoniously dumped into a bath tub filled with ice. "Fatal?" he asked. "Like in dying fatal?"

His grandfather nodded. "Exactly," he said, "with emphasis on the dying and the fatal." He opened the palm of his right hand and gestured that Will should place the tiny scimitars there. "There's one each for you and your friends," he said then smiling. "Each one has a wish attached; one for each of you thieves." His grandfather's smile vanished. "Use the wishes wisely," he said slowly. "They're not to be experimented with and they're not to be wasted." He gave a pause and then continued, this time even more slowly and seriously than he had ever talked with his grandson before. "I'm sure you've heard of Superman," he started.

"Yeah, Grandpa," interrupted Will. "I know. More powerful than a locomotive, faster than a speeding bullet and able to leap tall buildings in a single bound. Yeah, Grandpa, I know."

His grandfather's eyes seemed to bore into Will and he held out the innocent looking scimitars in the palm of his hand. "Will," he started out, "I can't make this any simpler for you so listen and listen good."

Will tried to nod, but his body wouldn't cooperate.

"Superman couldn't handle one of these on his best day," his grandfather said. He cleared his throat and began to explain the cautions attached to the miniature scimitars. "I learned all about the mysteries of the Middle East on my last Navy cruise in the Persian Gulf. I was only there for a short time because my hitch was up and I was about to be getting discharged. But, I learned more than enough."

After the cautions had been presented, Will felt a warmth return to his body. He saw his grandfather slide his chair away from the table and he knew it was time to head up to his attic bedroom. When he reached the attic stairs he heard his grandfather say, "Sleep tight, Will, and don't let the bed bugs bite."

There was the sound of light switch clicking on and Will started up the stairs his book and the four magical scimitars stuck firmly inside the front cover. He didn't see his grandfather's smile. He heard the kitchen light click off, but he was having trouble getting his feet to navigate the stairs. When he finally got up to his tiny room he was having trouble walking toward his bed. His body was still not cooperating and his palm, the one holding the book and the scimitars, was covered in a chilled sweat. Will didn't know how he managed to get under the bed covers. All that kept racing through his mind was telling his friends about the scimitars, the magic they possessed and his grandfather's warnings.   Then he noticed the book his grandfather had given him. It was open and the four scimitars seemed to be looking up at him.

Chapter 3
Inseparable Thieves

Will had propped his pillow against the wall behind his head, his bed minus a headboard, and he carefully picked up each of the four scimitars glistening on the open white page of the book. The scimitars seemed to beckon to him. He carefully placed each one on his night stand in a precision alignment. Then he turned his attention back to the book. His eyes slowly traveled down the page that was headed, INDEX as if he was afraid of missing even a letter. The story titles intrigued him more than any of the Howard Pease stories he had devoured. His mind fired off question after question curious about Sinbad the Sailor and Ali Baba. What and who were the forty thieves? Sinbad sailed on seas that Todd Moran never even heard of on his adventures. How would Sinbad have handled being a crewman on a tramp steamer?

Will's eye lids felt as if they weighed a ton, but sleep wouldn't come. When he felt himself about to doze off, he placed one of the scimitars back in the book using it as a bookmark. He had placed the four-shiny sticking down into the book so he wouldn't accidentally stick himself again. He tried to read but the wording, the way the story was being told wasn't like the English he had learned in school. Impatient, he started paging through the thick book, his fingers carefully turning each page, his eyes searching for a key word, a phrase, something that would grab him. Then he saw it. He felt his earlier ice bath turn into a solid block almost crushing him. A strange name jumped out of the page and seemed to penetrate his body.

*****

Will heard his name being called by his father. It was time for school and Will was always slow to get up and get going on school days. He glanced down and saw his book closed the cover face down on his chest. The handles of the four miniature scimitars were sticking out from top. Without thinking he opened the book to the last scimitar that he had used as a book mark. As he did, he realized that he had gone through the tale of Ali Baba and five of Sinbad's seven voyages before dozing off into a dream world of hideous flesh-eating monsters, giant birds, snakes that could devour elephants and a mysterious girl who poured hot oil over thieves to save innocent people. Todd Moran never encountered such adventures. Will felt a surge of energy and was out of bed as if launched by a medieval catapult. "The guys ain't ever gonna believe those scimitars my grandpa gave me," he said as he pulled on a blue crew neck sweater over a short sleeve white shirt with a button-down collar. "Boy, are they gonna crap when I lay grandpa's warnings on them." Still moving faster than he ever had getting ready for school he almost tripped and fell down the attic stairs after he had wrestled with uncooperative jeans that had stuck around his knees.

"Good morning," he muttered to his grandmother while giving her a hug, his enthusiasm almost knocking a spoon full of oat meal from her hand. He then turned his attention to his grandfather.

"What in tar nation," he heard his grandmother say as he gave his grandfather a hug. "Wow, Grandpa," he said, his enthusiasm still at full tilt. "That Sinbad the Sailor guy sure did meet some scary dudes on those voyages of his," he said gasping for breath.

"And, that Ali Baba guy and his sesame warning were awesome."

"You read 'em all already?" his grandfather asked.

"Only five voyages and Ali Baba, Grandpa," he said, his statement followed by his gulping down a glass of orange juice and jamming a way too full table spoon of oat meal into his mouth. He smacked his lips and his curled right index finger did a swiping motion at the corners of his mouth wiping off what seemed like an entire bowl of oat meal.

"Easy, Will," his father said as he set down his coffee cup on the table. "Take a moment to breath and chew. If you don't, you might end up choking to death."

"I'm fine, Dad," said Will. "Just in a hurry to get to school"

Will's father looked at Will's grandfather. "What was in that book you gave my son last night? Magic?"

"Kind of," Will's grandfather replied softly, almost cautiously. "I'll teach him some more magic when he gets home from school this afternoon." He gave his grandson a serious look. "I'm going to give you a brief lesson in being a Navy Signalman," he said. "Did you ever hear of a semaphore?"

"No, I haven't, Grandpa," said Will as he pushed his chair away from the table.

"I'll show you how to signal an S.O.S.," his grandfather continued. "Might save your life someday."

Will was up from his chair, his cereal spoon still stuck in his mouth. "Gotta split," he managed to say through a wad of oat meal and a metal spoon. He grabbed his bowl and placed it in the sink along with his spoon. He was almost running and about out the front door when he turned and shouted to his grandfather. "But, I'm sure you'll tell me all about it when I get home."

"That I will, Mister Book Worm. That I will."

They all heard the door slam shut.

"Well, whatever you did this is a first for my son and your grandson," his father said then pausing. He cleared his throat and said, "When have you ever seen the Book Worm in a hurry to get to school?'

Will's grandfather shrugged while his grandmother continued to savor her oat meal.

"Remember what I told you about those toothpicks," Will's grandfather said silently.

Chapter 4
Scimitar Warnings

Lunch and Recess were the only times during the school day that the four friends had time to spend together. All of them took the same classes their last year at Thorpe, advanced and honor level courses for the brightest at the Chicago Public School, but courses, time slots, teacher schedules and budget constraints had the four apart during the day. Will decided to wait until after school to show his friends what his grandfather had given them.

"These are so cool," he started out telling the others in the lunchroom where they always sat stuffed into a corner where they were almost hidden from the other kids. "How 'bout we meet in the playground by the softball backstop after school and I'll show you," he continued his eyes wide and excited.

"Okay," said Royal. "But, make it fast. I've got basketball practice."

"And, my Gram wants me home to help her carry some stuff down the basement for her," said Shakers. "I don't want to be late or she'll be yelling at me all week in Spanish."

"No problem, guys," said Will unable to curb his enthusiasm. "I don't need more than five minutes."

*****

Shakers, Royal and Chief sat on three of the four swings in the playground, the fourth dangling useless by a broken chain. Will was still in front of them, his own tiny scimitar held between his right thumb and forefinger. The others carefully examined their strange new gifts, Shakers sucking on his thumb where he had pricked it with the sharp point. For a rare time, the four were silent seemingly engrossed in the warnings that Will had conveyed from his grandfather. It was Chief who broke the silence. "Our medicine men couldn't come up with a bigger pile of bull crap than you and your grandfather just heaped on us," he said.

"El Toro poo-poo," muttered Shakers.

"The same goes for my father's camels," said Royal. She slid off the chipped wooden swing seat. "I gotta get to basketball practice," she said. "I don't want the coach mad at me."

"Before you go," Will said trying not to panic. "Is there any chance we can get together tonight at my house?"

"You know I can't get out on a school night," said Royal. "You know how strict my dad is." Her head went from side to side. "And, my mom's even worse," she quickly added.

"Would either of your parents buy into our coming over for a study session?" said Will trying desperately to find more time to explain the magic of the scimitars and the warning behind them.

"Call me," said Royal as she turned to jog back into the gym entrance to the school. "I'll let you know."

"You guys up to it?" asked Will of the others.

A pair of noncommittal grunts was the reply.

"Okay, I'll give each of you a call after I talk to Royal," he said.

"Study, huh," remarked Chief. "My parents will really believe that." He laughed. "I'm going to study at a girl's house." Another laughed escaped him. "That's rich."

"Royal ain't no girl," said Will. "She's a musketeer. She's one of the Sibs; one of us."

"Gram ain't gonna like this," said Shakers, his head going

from side to side as he wrapped his arms around the chain links of his swing.

"Ah, come on," said Will. "Your gram likes Royal. Didn't she once tell you she's as pretty as any girl from Puerto Rico?"

"And, smarter," snapped Chief. "Heck, she's smarter than three of us combined."

Will clapped his hands together. "Exactly, guys," he said almost shouting, "And that's why the three of us are going over to the house of the smartest girl in school for a study session."

*****

"What's with you and that cell phone thing of yours?" Will heard his grandfather ask as he ended his call with Ricky.

"Big test coming up, Grandpa," he replied as he slid the phone into his back pocket, a habit he was trying to break after cracking the screen on his phone one too many times and not having the money to repair it. "The thieves, as you call us, are setting up a study group for this evening at Farah's house." He paused and then added, "Both her parents thought it was a good idea."

Will could see his grandfather's skeptical eyes giving him the once over. A subdued grunt came from him. "That girl gets straight A's," he said before delivering the real meaning behind the remarks that followed. "Why would she want to study with three dumbkopfs?" He grinned. "Thank god you're not like those two buddies of yours who have been rejected for brain transplants."

"Ah, come on, Grandpa," stated Will trying to keep the conversation from heating up which most conversations with his grandfather did when his friends were mentioned. "You gave me the opportunity to read when you gave me that Howard Peace book and look what happened to my grades," he said adding a pause filled with pride. "I'm going to Lane Teach and Lane don't take no transplant candidates."

"Doesn't take," Will's grandfather added.

"Right," replied Will. "We just want to ace those big tests coming up and we want to help one another."

His grandfather gave a nod. "Helping one another is good," he said. "Not enough of that going on in the world today." He paused and gave a second identical grunt. "Just remember about that helping stuff in the future especially if you give each of your friends one of those magical scimitars I gave you."

Will saw his grandfather's eyes grow more intense; a danger signal was flashing. "I showed them the scimitars in the playground after school today." He thought for a moment. "I only showed them grandpa," he said weighing each word. He paused again. "Well, I did tell them about the warnings." He saw his grandfather's eyebrows go up slightly. "I don't think they believed me."

His grandfather's eye brows raised even more. "They'd better," he warned.

"I'll be sure they understand the warning before I give each of the Thieves their scimitars tonight when we finish our study session, Grandpa." He stopped and thought for a moment. "I'll really warn them, Grandpa," he said. "Just the way you warned me."

"Good," his grandfather muttered. "Now, are you ready to learn how to give an S.O.S. signal with your hands and arms?"

"Do I have to, Grandpa?"

He did.

*****

Will, Robert and Ricky walked together to where Farah lived.

Her house was a small, square Georgian with a big flagstone rock garden across the front; a gang of yews in desperate need of pruning spilling over the stone. This was the first time any of them had been invited inside their friend's house and they didn't know what to expect. As Will rang the front door bell he turned to Robert and Ricky and warned, "Manners, guys."

"Right, Mister Etiquette Man," said Robert. "Like us guys who come from Puerto Rico don't have no manners."

"Yeah," hissed Ricky. "Us Native Americans ain't nothin' but savages to you pale face types who speak with forked tongue."

"Just be polite," said Will as the front door opened and they stood looking up at a giant of a man who had to be Farah's father.

Giant of a man may have been a misnomer to describe Wally Smolinski, Farah's father. Tall he definitely was, well over six foot three, and he did fill in the front door entrance way so not even a ray of light could squeeze through. In reality, his body resembled an apple on stilts with all of the fruit's shape centered from just below his sternum to below his belt. His neck resembled a modified stork that had trouble holding up his oversize head. He sported a tough, square jaw and a nose that had several curves. His one major weakness was glowing, kind blue eyes. Any other weaknesses he may have had were minimized by a gravel voice that sported the foulest of language, but never at home. His vulgar communication skills were reserved strictly for the loading dock at the meat packing company where he worked and while loading and unloading his truck. Walter Smolinski adored his wife and daughter and was an old-fashioned protector of his family; defending to the death the only two women in his life.

"Good evening, Mister Smolinski," said Will politely with a

touch of masculine forcefulness he had learned from his grandfather when addressing elders. "Farah invited us over for a study session. I hope that's okay." He reached out to shake the huge man's hand and then wished he hadn't.

"Ah," grunted Farah's father, his massive hand appearing to crush Will's hand if smashing a bag of potato chips. He sounded both bored and sarcastic. "Numer Jeden, Numer Dwa and Trzy, the Three Stooges," he said, counting to three in his native Polish tongue. "You three are here to help my daughter get smarter, right?"

Will swallowed hard by never lost polite eye contact even though he had no feeling in his hand. "No, sir," he said. "We're here to help us get smarter with the help of your daughter. She's the smartest person in the school," he continued without stopping. "She's smarter than most of the teachers and ...." He stopped when he saw the massive right hand of Farah's father release his own hand and go up as if he were giving a signal to halt traffic.

"Come on in," said Farah's father, his movement out of the door appearing to make the noise of a cork being removed from a bottle. "My daughter's expecting you," he said shaking his head from side to side several times. "I don't know why. When I opened the door all I could see were three glowing cell phone screens. You three guys looked like a trio of fire flies," he said, his head going from side to side.

"The phones will be turned off and put away, sir," said Will as he led his two friends into the living room of the house that blinked average middleclass American like a red, white and blue flashing neon sign. "And thank you and Farah's mother for allowing us to come over for a study session."

"It's just like my grandmother's living room," Shakers whispered over his shoulder to Chief.

"A very cool wigwam," replied Chief back. "Just like a couple of those magazines about houses and gardens my mother's always reading."

The three stopped in the middle of the living room when they saw their friend, Royal. She was seated on a chocolate brown leather sofa next to her mother. Three sets of eyes were frozen on Royal's mother. This was the first time they had ever seen her in person and a series of identical thoughts went through their heads. "Royal's mother was indeed from royalty. Royal's mother didn't look like a mother. Royal's mother should have been," according to Will's thoughts, "ruling a country in a *Thousand and One Nights*. Each of the boys gave a respectful nod.

"Welcome, boys," said Royal's mother, a slight foreign accent to her voice that sounded from a land far, far away. "Farah thought it would be a good idea if you all studied in here, and I agreed with her. Make yourself comfortable. Farah's father and I will be in the kitchen if you need anything."

The three watched Farah's mother get up as if she were rising from her throne.

Not knowing what to do or say, Will replied, "Thank you, Mam."

Chief mumble something that sounded like, "Yeah, thanks."

Shakers simply nodded.

The three watched Royal's parents leave the room, each of them thinking: "How could a queen be escorted into the kitchen by a court jester who really did look like a giant apple on stilts.

*****

Will was having trouble concentrating on the test review even though Royal was a great instructor and tutor. Before an hour had ended he was feigning a yawn with an exaggerated stretch and stating: "How 'bout we take a little break." He gave a second yawn and stretch for affect and said, "Remember those tiny swords I showed you guys in the playground that you all thought were fancy toothpicks and you made fun of them?"

Mixed muffled grumbling came from the other three.

"Really?" asked Royal, her eyebrows raised. "How many more stories do you have for us about those silly looking toothpicks?" she asked. "Shame on you for telling us that your grandfather was responsible for that big fairy tale you tried to get us to believe."

"You have more magic than an Ojibwa medicine man," said Chief, his head going back and a yawn escaping his wide-open mouth. "Hey, guys, we get a lucky tooth pick that has a magic wish attached." He glared at Will. "Is that magic some kind of dental floss?"

Royal smiled at Will. Secretly she had a crush on him but never told a soul. "Oh, let him tell us about his grandfather's magical scimitars," she said to the others, her smile not changing. "His grandfather's not into voodoo or black magic or anything like that," she continued.

"And how do you know that?" asked Shakers.

"It's logical," said Royal.

"Since when is bad medicine logical?" shot back Chief.

"I told my grandmother about those wishes and the warnings Will gave us the last time and she started humming some of her church hymns and looking really concerned," said Shakers.

The room turned quiet until Will stated: "Look, guys, none of this works until we each have one of those scimitars in our hand

and vow that we will only make a wish that will do good. None of this getting rich quick like in the lottery games; or getting a fancy car that most people only dream about or getting even with someone who gives you a rough time whenever you're around them."

Shakers let out a laugh. "Like my English teacher, Miss Boop who thinks she's a Playboy Playmate."

"What do you know about Playboy Playmates?" asked Chief taking a step closer to Shakers. "You're not old enough to buy any of those girlie magazines."

"I didn't buy a thing," shot back Shakers. "My dad would forget and leave a copy lying around the house occasionally. It drove my mom nuts. Me, on the other hand, couldn't be bothered with that kind of stuff."

"Good for you, Shakers," said Royal finally taking her eyes off Will. "Those pictures are so demeaning of women."

"Then why do they pose for that stuff?" asked Chief.

"Come on, guys be serious," said Will as he slowly waved his right hand back and forth to get the others' attention. "Look, guys, each of us will have a wish. We can use it on what we want. We just have to be careful that's all," he said trying to warm each of his friends. "When we take the pledge my grandfather gave us," he continued growing more serious, "we have to follow it to the letter." He paused and glanced at each of his friends. "It's so simple it's almost stupid. But, if you treat the pledge as a joke, and these are my grandfather's exact words, "You'll wish you were never born."

Silence engulfed the room, the only sound coming from a small television in the kitchen where Royal's parents were seated. Will handed out the tiny scimitars to each of his friends, the last one going into the palm of his right hand. "Are we in this together?" he asked. "You know, the one for all and all for one with no, and I go first."

No one spoke. Three sets of eyes glanced at three open right-hand palms. Will was the exception. He was too occupied with getting everything his grandfather had told him; the warnings, the quote and the explanations correct. He wasn't about to mess up.

*****

Three sets of astonished eyes questioned Will and he wasn't sure how to respond. He finally said: "You guys gotta believe my grandfather even if you don't appear to believe me." His own eyes shifted back and forth looking for any kind of response. He got none.

"Just why in the world did your grandfather give these to you and us?" asked Royal.

"Yeah, Worm, why?" asked Chief.

"What gives?" asked Shakers.

"Grandpa just thinks there's too much craziness in the world today. He wanted each of us to be safe. I guess so we could have something to rely on if we ever faced an emergency."

The other three appeared to believe him.

"My grandfather isn't the kind of guy who would make this stuff up," he continued cautiously feeling he was about to crack through a thin sheet of ice that was making creaking and popping sounds all around him. "He told me about the vow we would have to make. He even showed me the sign language we could use in an emergency. I told you he was in the Navy and he said that as part of their training in Navy boot camp they had to learn how to signal," he said, then stopping to think. "Oh, yeah, he called it a semaphore. That's what it was. It was a series of hand signals. He rattled them off like he was still in boot camp." He looked at his friends and still didn't get a response. "You guys all heard of the emergency signal. S.O.S., I know you have."

Three heads barely nodded.

"Doesn't that mean, save our ship?" said Shakers softly.

"I heard, save our soul," said Royal.

Chief gave a smile. "More like, save our skin."

The three friends appeared glued in place until Chief blinked and looked at the others. He then looked at Will with a facial expression that left no doubt as to what was coming. "Worm," he started out, "like I told you in the playground, that's the biggest load of crap I've ever heard." He glanced at Royal. "I apologize for my language," he continued. "I hope your parents didn't hear me. I know if mine did, I'd get whipped with blackberry briars to within an inch of my life."

"No, you wouldn't," said Royal with a pleasant smile. "I've met your parents. Your mom's like mine and your dad is like my dad; lots of bark and no bite."

"Let me show you the fang marks," Chief replied. He turned his attention back to Will but before he could say anything, Shakers spoke.

"El Toro poo-poo, Worm," he said sarcastically. "You want us to believe we each have a magical wish; one that would protect us and keep us safe from danger? Then, if we don't use it the right way, it could be fatal? That is, fatal in kill us." He swallowed then continued. "You've got to be making all of this stuff up," he said. "I know your grandfather and he'd never dump a load of whatever Royal's dad calls it in Polish on us."

"That's crap," interjected Chief. "Pure crap in any language"

He was staring at Will in disbelief. "Vows," he repeated. "Will, we ain't getting married. This ain't our birthdays so, we don't get any wishes. And, survival signals so we can be rescued." He stopped cold while continuing to stare. "What do I look like, a traffic cop?"

Royal smiled at Will. "You're joking, right?" she asked. "I know that's not what you do, you being kind of shy and all of that." Her smiled continue to be warm and friendly. "I really like the tiny scimitars you gave us," she then continued, displaying the miniature sword between her thumb and forefinger. "They're kind of cute." She paused and then said what she wished she hadn't. "Kind of like you, Will."

Shakers and Chief felt their jaws drop.

"Oh, guys," she said noticing the expressions. "I was just teasing. You know we're all friends. You know, like Will always says, all for one and one for all." She took a quick glance at her friends. "That's right, Will, isn't it? You know, the one for all and all for one thing you always preach."

"Yeah," replied Will trying not to stammer. "I really wish you'd believe me about what my grandfather told me," he continued. "He gave me this book to read and it had all kinds of neat stories," he said, then pausing. "It was about someone named Ali Baba and there were these forty thieves who wanted to kill him." He paused again and displayed his scimitar. "They were going to use the bigger versions of this tiny guy," he said while slowly twirling the scimitar between his thumb and forefinger. "Then some slave girl saved him and he lived happily ever after."

"I know the story," said Royal. "My mother told me about it when I was a little girl. It took place in a place not too far from where my relatives were from. It was a city called Baghdad."

"I heart of that," said Shakers. "Ain't that the place where people zoom around on flying carpets?"

"Oh, brother," Chief interrupted. "My people can tell all kinds of stories about evil spirits and good and bad medicine, but slave girls, rugs that fly and a place called Baghdad. Geez."

Will looked at his friends. "How 'bout we at least take the vow," he said, coaxing them to place the scimitars in the palms of their hands. "There ain't no wishes without the vow," he said continuing carefully, almost pleading. "And, we only get one wish each."

"What happened to, one for all," asked Chief who was carefully rotating his scimitar between his thumb and forefinger, his eyes examining.

"One for all ain't going anywhere," said Will, trying not to show he was getting frustrated. "Anyway, what's there to be afraid of? You guys ain't scaredy cats, are you?"

"Of course not," said Royal. She held out her right hand, palm up and placed her scimitar in it. "See," she said sounding brave and bold at the same time. Girls aren't afraid of vows like you boys." She lost her battle and let out a giggle.

Shakers held out his hand, palm up and placed his scimitar in it. "Big deal, Will," he said. "Get on with the vow routine of yours."

Chief gave a shrug. "Count me in," he said sounding disgusted. "This is still a big pile of horse manure but, I'm one of the musketeers and I'm loyal."

Will looked at each one of his friends. "Are you guys sure?"

Three heads nodded; three hands were still held out, the tiny, shining scimitars appearing harmless.

Just then Royal's father walked into the room. "Looks like your brain surgeon session is about to be called on account of rain," he said seriously. "Farah's mother and I just got the severe weather bulletin on the television. Looks like a dandy's moving in and going to dump on us."

The four friends looked at one another. Then Will, hiding his depression as best he could which wasn't very good, said. "We can finish the story on the front porch. Then it's each man for himself. Heck, it's only rain and I know Chief and Shakers ain't gonna melt."

Laughter filled the room and Royal's father led them to the front door. "No dilly dallying around," he warned. "There are heavy lightning and thunder warnings with this storm," he continued. He opened the front door and stepped aside so the three boys could get out on the front porch.

"Thanks, Daddy," Royal said to her father. "I'll get the door."

Her father stepped aside and said, "Make the goodbyes quick." I don't want to see any of your friends getting zapped with a bolt of lightning."

"We'll be okay," Mister S," said Chief. He was sandwiched in between Worm and Shakers with Royal pushing against the metal storm door with her right side keeping it open.

"Thanks, Mister Smolinski," said Shakers. "Don't worry. We'll out run the rain. We all live just a couple of blocks away."

Royal's father didn't linger and was back inside. Will once again could feel the icy chill settle into him. "Now remember, guys," he started out, his voice in a command that none of the others had ever heard, and that included Will. "You've got to repeat the vow exactly as I give it. No messing around. No game playing. No joking."

Lightning lit up the sky to the southwest. Suddenly a giant clap of thunder exploded almost knocking them off the porch.

"You guys okay?" asked Will, his eyes focused on the threatening sky and then shifting to the others. "Come on, we can get this done in a second."

"You already told us about being serious and no game playing," said Royal. "Get on with it."

"Yeah," said Chief. "We understand what the letters 'n' and 'o' mean. "We're not stupid."

"We'll repeat your grandfather's words exactly as you say them, Will," replied Royal, She noticed that her hand was beginning to tremble.

"On with it," Worm," said Robert. "I'm already late getting home and my grandmother will have some of her choice Spanish words for me if I come in looking like a drowned rat."

"Yeah, Worm, get 'er done," said Chief.

"Okay," said Will, holding his own hand out, the scimitar glistening. "Just be sure that the scimitar is pointing at your heart." He paused then quickly added. "And no jokes."

All the hands were trembling when the entire neighborhood lit up as if a giant fire bomb had been dropped there.

Chapter 5
Flying Carpets

Will was proud of himself that the vow went off perfectly. When they had finished they, all looked at one another wondering what was next. They didn't have to wait long. There was a blinding flash followed by an explosion of thunder that made their ears ring and sent a sharp pain through the heads of each as if the scimitars had been poked in between their eyes. Four pairs of hands shot up to cover their faces.

"Geez, Chief," said Will, his words filtered through his fingertips. "I hope you didn't go and do some insane prank of yours like ignoring my grandpa and making a wish?"

"Right," replied Chief, his words barely squirming through the palms of his hands. "When in doubt blame the Indian." He gritted his teeth and muttered, "Damn, that hurts."

The four-young friends started to remove their hands from their respective faces when another ear-splitting explosion followed. Then the heavens opened and they felt themselves being swept off the front porch.

Shakers was the last one who managed to say a word. "My Gramma's gonna kill me when I get home."

*****

The four friends were huddled together in a tight circle kneeling on the ground. But it wasn't the ground they knew in the Thorpe School playground, and it wasn't the lawn in front of Royal's parent's house. This ground was sand and they weren't surrounded by their friends. They weren't surrounded by anyone they knew. These were the strangest people they had ever seen. These strange people dressed strange; they looked strange and the surroundings were strange.

"Geez," muttered Will, his voice in a whisper as he was too fearful of drawing attention to the four of them. Four-young people kneeling in a tight circle in a crowd drew more than attention. Stares, questioning looks and a few passersby stopped to look, but only for a moment as if staring was against the law. Expressionless, not curious enough and not wanting to be bothered, each person moved on.

"Where are we?" whispered Shakers.

"Beats me," Chief chimed in looking at the others for help. He shrugged because he didn't know what else to do. "You can't blame the Indians," he whispered like the others. "It's got to be the cowboys or the cavalry."

Will knew immediately what had happened and all but glared at Shakers and Chief. "Okay," he said his voice a mix between showing disgust, anger and fear. "Which one of you two morons used up a wish? Who did it?"

Chief and Shakers had identical looks on their faces saying: "What are you talking about, Worm?"

"Well," said Will, his hands on his hips; his mixed feelings whirling almost out of control. "Who used a wish?"

"Why are you accusing us?" asked Chief. "I sure as heck didn't use up any stupid wish."

"Me neither," said Shakers. "I took a vow."

Silence settled in amongst the four as passersby stopped, gawked and then went on their way. It was a scene that the four had only seen in old movies on a station that specialized in classic movies from way before the four were born; even before some of their parents were born or were still in diapers. One thing for certain, they weren't in Chicago. Where they were at was different from anyplace any of them had been before.

"Where in the hell are we at?" asked Chief, his nerves showing they were taking him over and shoving away his cocky attitude.

"We're in an Arab bazaar," said Royal softly sounding timid. Then tears started streaming down her cheeks. "It was me, Will," she stammered. "I'm the one who made the wish. I just wanted to see if what you told us was for real. I thought it would be fun to go a land that had flying carpets so Shakers and Chief could see for themselves.   A land my mother told me about." Forefingers wiped away some of the tears. "I'm so sorry, Will," she managed to choke out. "Please forgive me."

Will gave a nod and tried to force a smile. His lips seemed frozen. "Nothing to forgive," he said, another nod coming. "At least we know my grandfather wasn't putting us on. He's been known to do that." His lips now began to curl at the corners. "Hey, and we still have three wishes left." His hands went palms up and pointed at Chief and Shakers. "Don't even think about it."

"We're not stupid," said Shakers. He glanced at Royal. "Not like Miss Brains over there."

Royal started to cry again.

Will scooted across the sand on his knees and was by Royal's side. He put his arm around her shoulder. "Nothing to cry about," he said, giving her shoulder a gentle squeeze. "Where do you think we're at?"

Royal sniffled and then said, "Baghdad."

Three jaws dropped.

"Bag what?" asked Chief when feeling finally came back to his body.

"As in that flying carpet place?" asked Shakers not wanting to turn his head and look around in fear that the strange people who had stopped to give them a glance before moving on, would not move on and turn into a mob. "Hey, guys," he whispered cautiously, "I don't know if you noticed it or not, but more and more people are stopping to stare at us and they ain't moving on," he said, his eyes shifting back and forth at the growing number of people beginning to surround them. "I think I'm seeing the start of a street gang forming, and you know what happens when a bunch of gang bangers gets out of hand."

"I think I know exactly what you're getting at," said Royal, looking at the crowd around them, questioning looks being cast at them.

"Really?" asked Will. "Of all people, you're worried about a handful of people staring at us?"

Royal's head went up and down once.

"Really?" asked Will again not noticing that Chief and Shakers had shifted closer to Royal. "I was kind of hoping you were going to show us those flying carpets, Ali Baba and thieves with scimitars and maybe Aladdin and his lamp." He tried to smile and then saw the crowd had tripled in sized. The expressions on their faces were no longer curious.

Will slowly slipped his cell phone out of his back pocket. "How 'bout we try a little local nine-one-one," he whispered to the others. His thumbs were a blur. He glanced at his phone and then at the others. He glanced at his phone again. "I'm not getting any bars," he muttered sounding frustrated, his thumbs poking at the screen.

"I don't think our cell phones are going to work here," said Royal trying to stay calm. She gave a slight nod. "Will," she said trying not to panic.

"I think the four of us should start walking and get away from this crowd. I don't like what I'm seeing or feeling." Her eyes made contact with his and then the others. "Will, you lead the way. And, please, stand up real slow and then walk like you don't want to get to school too early. We don't want to give these people something to get nervous about."

"What way?" asked Will trying to stay calm as he got to his feet.

There was the sound of a murmur from the crowd.

"I don't know where I'm at and all of these people dressed in what looks like their bed sheets don't have very friendly looks on their faces. I think they might be getting a bit nervous; just like you said."

"There's a street behind you," she said, still staying calm. "Well, it looks like a street. It's more of what we know as an alley. These bazaars are honeycombed with them. Just head to the one on your right and the rest of us will follow you. I'll bring up the rear like a good Arab woman would. I learned that from my mother who, by the way, wouldn't bring up the rear to any man."

Before they had been noticed by the local people they had been huddled together, squatting and bent over. When they stood up the crowd that had gathered backed away, a sound of awe coming from them. It didn't take long for the three boys to figure out what had happened. Royal stood almost a head taller than they were. Farah Smolinski stood out, well, like a royal princess.

Will turned and slowly led the way knowing that more eyes that he had ever seen were boring holes in him and his friends. What he didn't realize was that the seas of eyes had never seen anyone dressed in running shoes, jeans and t-shirts sporting various athletic teams. The four would stand out wherever they went.

The narrow street that Will led them into was lined on both sides with booths and stalls stacked with various goods that appeared for sale. Merchants and buyers bargained in loud voices.

"They're haggling," said Royal, her voice now calm and the only trace of her crying in the form of two dusty ridges on her cheeks. "It's what Arabs love to do."

"Just as long as they're not bargaining to see which one of us ends up being their slave," said Chief. "Us Ojibwa were shafted by the Great White Father in Washington once upon a time and I don't want to end up on the sharp end of one of those pig stickers jammed at me by a guy who wears a towel around his head."

"Just keep following Will," Royal urged. "No one cares who we are now."

So, she thought.

*****

Royal was at the end of the line being led by Worm; Chief and Shakers were right behind him breathing down his neck. Royal kept whispering commands about when and where to turn; the commands passed forward to Will. He led them through the maze of narrow like alleys that varied in width to Chicago neighborhood streets to their shoulders brushing up against stone walls. They trusted Royal's directions from the back of the pack. Worm, Chief and Shakers all surmised that if Royal had any of her mother's ancestor's royal blood, they would be led to safety.

The problem soon appeared that safety didn't appear to be in sight. They were in a country surrounded by sand and inhabited by women who wore a veil across their faces and men looking like their heads were covered with what appeared to be pillow cases. Their feelings of being safe were slowly turning into the sand they trod on.

Royal gave a whispered command and they stopped to rest in a small alcove cut back from the main alley by a length no longer than any one of them. The hot sun was blocked by what looked like the outside wall of a building. There were no doors or windows and the only evidence of someone having been there was the remains of what they thought might have been a peddler's stand. The four sat down, backs against the wall unable to see in either direction of what or who might be coming in the alley.

"Guys," Royal started to say and then burst into tears. "I'm really sorry about the wish and getting us into this mess."

Before she could continue, Will interrupted her. "We're not in any mess," he said trying to reassure him as well as the others. "Hey, look at all of this on the positive side," he continued. "We know the wish thing works." He glanced at the others. "You know, one for all and all for one."

"Big deal," said Chief as he thrust his legs out to stretch. "We're here in a place not even my tribe's best scout or even a corps of our medicine men could find. And, our chiefs and elders wouldn't know what to do with so much sand." He paused and looked at the others. "We're in a weird looking city where a couple of us think people fly around on carpets and, for all we know they rub magic lamps and make wishes we can if we need to."

The group grew silent except for Royal who continued to weep, her hands covering her face.

"Okay," said Will. He was trying to be authoritative but the others weren't listening. "Remember, we still have three wishes left. If one of those wishes got us in here then one of the remaining wishes can get us out of here." He glanced at the others and saw Royal lower her hands. Will's eyes asked the simple question.

Nods came from the other three.

"I'd kind of like to see if there are any of those flying carpets zooming over the roof tops of these strange looking buildings." His head went back as if were scanning the sky. "If we get in a jam, we can always use up a wish, grab a rug and fly back to Chicago."

"Shakers is right," said Will as he got up to his knees and sat back on his heels. "Just remember though, Royal used her wish." He paused and looked at Shakers and Chief. "We still got ours."

"I didn't mean to," Royal started to say as the shadow of what appeared to be a man walked by the tiny alcove where they were resting and trying to figure out what to do next. "Oh, my gosh," she blurted out, her right hand in a fist going to her mouth. "I know that man."

"You what?" the other three asked, their heads turning to the alley. There was no one there.

"I thought I recognized that man who just walked by," she said, her fist still to her mouth. "I saw his picture in a scrapbook my mother has of her family and relatives when they lived in Iran."

"Don't joke with us, Royal," warned Chief. "Blowing a wish on getting us into this mess was bad enough; now you know one of these characters?"

"Yeah," added Shakers, his head still turned to the alley. "And all of those characters have looks on their faces like they want to string us up the way they did in the movies I saw at the Will Rogers and the Patio." He glanced back at the others. "I don't like this one bit."

"Easy, guys," said Will calmly, scooting over to Royal. He was about to put his arm around her shoulder when they were all startled by a man's voice. He spoke English.

"Forgive me, your Royal Highness," the man said with a respectful bow. "I thought I recognized you."

"You did?" replied Royal, a nervous surprise coating her response.

"Yes, your Royal Highness," the man continued. His head was shifting nervously back and forth. "You're in danger and I'm here to protect you and guide you to safety.

The look that each of the four wore on their face asked a multitude of questions; none of them good and the answers even worse.

"I don't understand," said Royal.

The man looked in both directions in the alley and then held out his hand. In his other hand was a cloth bag that was a bit smaller than something the four friends' parents would carry home from the supermarket. "Please, your Royal Highness. You and your entourage must come with me before it's too late."

Chief and Shakers had gotten to their feet and were gawking at the man. "Before what's too late?" asked Chief.

"Yeah," Shakers managed to get out as the man's hand, index

finger extended, went to his lips. He gave another nervous look at the alley and then reached out and took Royal by the hand.

"Forgive me, your majesty, but you all must come with me. Your lives are in danger."

Chief and Shakers glanced at each other and then at Will. "Lead the way," said Chief in a hushed voice without hesitating.

The Arab man pulled a veil out of the bag he carried and gave it to Royal indicating that she should put it across her face. Another garment appeared from the bag, a larger, heavier shawl like cloth that the man respectfully, almost reverently draped around her shoulders. "Be sure your face is covered," the man said cautiously. He quickly turned to the three boys and pulled what looked like large squares of cloth. He handed each a square. "These are a traditional keffiyeh worn by my people. Be sure your head is wrapped and the remainder hangs down over your shoulder covering those white things you wear."

"They're t-shirts," said Chief.

"Mine says University of Chicago," added Shakers. "That's where my parents worked before they were killed."

The man nodded as if he understood. "Cover yourself, your head, face and as much of your shoulders and chest as you can." He gave each a serious look. "I don't want you joining your parents."

"Really," repeated Shakers, suddenly realizing that wishes and miniature scimitars were no longer the tale of an old man; the old man being more than Worm's grandfather.

The man gave another nod. "I'm sure you've all heard of a scimitar," he said.

Four-young people felt a chill race through them. Shakers felt more than a chill.

"Good," the man said taking Royal's hand and leading them into the alley. "Follow close and don't stop for anything or anyone," he warned, his finger slowly wagging as it pointed at each of them. "And make no wishes."

Will glanced at the others, his eyes asking, "How did he know that?"

Chapter 6
Baba

They were walking stooped over and so close behind one another that they looked like a cloth dragon in a Chinese New Year's parade. Only this wasn't China and it wasn't a New Year's celebration. The four-young people had come to grips with the fact that their lives were in the hands of an old Arab man who knew so much about them, but they knew nothing about him. The old man suddenly stopped where the alley seemed to end at the beginning of a vast sand road. He put up his index finger to his lips as he looked at the four-young people behind him; his hand still holding Royal's, but in a respectful; protective way.

The four Musketeers looked up the road that was clogged with caravans and merchants hauling their wares in the direction of a massive stone structure protected by two massive wooden doors that were taller than the four of them if they stood on each other's shoulder.

"Is that a castle?" asked Worm feeling in awe.

"It is the Sultan's palace," answered the Arab.

"Palace," repeated Chief. "Cool, man."

Royal didn't have to look up at the man to talk. She was almost eye-to-eye with him. "Sir," she started out feeling a sense of power, a sense of leadership. "I," she started, then stopping and looking at the others. "We are most thankful that you have led us out of that maze back in the bazaar, but we don't even know your name."

"Baba," the man said. "I'm known as Baba, Baba the Tailor to the royal court where I serve his majesty the Sultan in many capacities." He gave a polite bow.

"Excuse me, Mister Baba," said Worm, but is that any relation to Ali Baba?"

The man's dark eyes gave a twinkle. "Ah, ha, my infidel friend, it appears you are versed in the ways and customs of my people," he said. He never stopped appearing on guard, at the ready, giving the impression that he was expecting to come under attack at any moment. "I am of the same bloodline as this Ali Baba you mention."

"Gee," said Worm not knowing what else to say.

"Now that's definitely cool, man," said Chief. "You gonna show us that Open Sesame place?"

Baba's index finger went to his lips, a look of admonishment cast at Chief.

"Alright, already," said Chief. He pinched his right index finger and thumb together and ran them along his lips from one side to the other and then back again. "My lips are sealed."

"Better your lips than you're holding your head in your hands," said the old man.

Chief's look asked his question.

Baba lowered his voice. "Your head is in your hands because it was removed from your neck by a scimitar."

"Definitely not cool," said Chief as he ran his thumb and forefinger across his lips several more times.

The sun was beginning to set and the four Musketeers noticed that there were fewer travelers heading toward the palace; those at a quickened pace almost as if racing toward safety. Only a scattering of stray figures spaced well apart were heading toward them and the sprawling city with its bazaar. They too walked at a faster pace.

"We need to hurry," said Baba, his eyes shifting more than ever. "When the sun's glow begins to vanish so does the safety of our surroundings," he said in hushed voice. He looked at the four. "Especially not for four infidels from the west," he said surprising them.

"How did you know where we were from?" asked Royal politely as she removed her hand from Baba's.

"Baba the Tailor knows many things," he said. He paused and looked back at the outside wall of the bazaar. "We must go quickly," he said, his words stern. "The sun is warning us to get to the safety of the palace if we value our lives," he continued, his statement sounding like an order. "It's too late to make it on foot." He glanced at Shakers. "You, Mister Robert, Junior will be enthralled by the mode of transportation I have in store for you and your companions." Baba let out a loud grunt as if he were calling a pet animal. Nothing happened. He grunted again. A cylindrical object shaped like a log and covered by a mound of dirt and sand moved from where it was piled against the wall. The object was about ten feet in length and eight feet wide and it surprised Worm, Chief, Shakers and Royal as it rolled away from the wall of the bazaar as if it were obeying Baba's strange sounding command. Billows of dirt and sand dust particles filled the air as if some giant animal was shaking its coat. Several more grunts, these more subdued, came from Baba and the large object began to unroll, to open up.

The four looked in awe at what turned out to be a large carpet complete with a fringe edging. What held their attention was that the carpet appeared to be floating about a foot off the ground.

"Quickly," ordered Baba pointing at the carpet. "Get on! We

have no time to waste."

"Is that what I think it is," said Shakers with a big grin. "Oh, man, Worm, your grandpa wasn't putting us on one bit. It's a real flying carpet."

Royal had followed Baba's order immediately and was situated in the center of the carpet. Worm followed and sat back on his heels next to her. Shakers, who wasn't about to miss the thrill of a lifetime, scampered onto the carpet and knelt in from of Worm and Royal and was facing forward. Baba stepped onto the carpet, but Chief wasn't moving.

"Come," said Baba, his order polite as he held out his hand to Chief.

"I ain't flying on no rug," said Chief. "My people travel by canoe, on horseback or by foot."

"Young, Mister Chief," said Baba. "Do you remember my mentioning scimitars and one's head in one's hand?"

Chief jumped on the carpet and sat down behind Worm and Royal.

Baba gave out another grunt. This was quickly joined by a single clap of his hands. The four friends couldn't believe what happened next as the carpet slowly lifted up higher and higher in a vertical climb until it was several hundred feet above the heads of the travelers on the road below.

"Oh, man, my Grandma Rios ain't ever gonna believe this," said Shakers as he leaned forward to get a better view. "Her grandson is sailing through the air on a flying carpet."

"She'll believe it when you fall off this thing," said Worm trying not to shout. "Scoot your butt back before you end up on the heads of those people below us."

Baba clapped his hands twice and the carpet began to move

forward until they were feeling a stiff breeze blowing in their faces. His eyes were fixed on the setting sun and growing shade of darkness creeping over the sand and hills. He clapped his hands again and muttered some words that none of them understood. The flying carpet appeared to understand, making a slight turn that put them in the direction of the palace with its high, foreboding walls.

"I ain't likin' this," said Chief, his eyes closed and his hands gripping at the short nap of the carpet as he tried to hang on. "Canoes and horses my people know. Rugs are made from bear and buffalo hides."

"I'm lovin' it," yelled Shakers. "Faster, Baba, go faster!"

Suddenly, there were a series of flashes.

"What the heck," said a startled Chief. Then he saw the reason for the flashes. There was a grinning Shakers holding his cell phone, the camera at the ready.

"My Grandma Rios never believes a word I say," he said confidently. "She'll believe these pictures of the palace and us flying over it."

Before they knew they were over the walls of the palace. They thought their eyes would pop out of their heads with what they saw below. The palace was a city within a city. Once inside the heavy wooden gates that were taller than all of them combined, there was a massive circle of shops and stalls circling half the palace. Small homes were joined together by common walls. Each had a small wooden door and no visible window in the front. There was a flaming torch in front of each house, the flame guiding the occupant home. Once inside, the flame was extinguished. Torches circled the other half of the palace grounds. Animals from the caravans they had seen earlier were tethered neat to their owners and numerous camp fires were beginning to sprout up like flickering lamps seeming to drive back the approaching night and keeping at bay what might be lurking in the approaching total blackout.

"Look at all those lights burning in that inner circle," said Worm to Royal.

"Lamps and torches," said Baba. "Electric lights are what you Westerners have, I believe," he continued, your lights are made of glass and you have a magic switch that you touch for them to go on. Is that not so?"

Worm was fascinated with the Arab man and his knowledge of another part of the world so far from his. "Baba," he started out feeling playful, "do you know everything about everywhere and everyone?"

"Master Will," said Baba respectfully, "I only know what I need to know." He clapped his hands three times as the flying carpet was above what appeared to be a vast garden surrounded by palm trees and punctuated with several glistening pools illuminated by more flaming torches. The carpet now hovered above an open grassy area and began to settle gently down.

"I hope you know how to land this thing," said Chief, his eyes open, but his hands still clutching at the carpet's surface. Just then the carpet settled softly on the grass with no evidence of a bump or jolt. Chief's knuckles felt the solid ground through the carpet and he started to get up when he felt Baba's hand on his arm.

"Manners, Master Chief," said Baba. "You are visitors and infidels and I need permission for you to touch this sacred ground."

Chief sat back on his heels saying nothing but looking for the nearest escape route and ready to use his wish.

"Is this where you live, Baba?" asked Royal.

"It is, Princess," replied Baba with a slight bow. "I serve at the pleasure of the Sultan in many capacities."

Just then a large muscular black man appeared through an opening in the hedges lining the clearing where they sat on the carpet. Baba left the carpet and walked up to the black man who was naked from the waist up except for a turban wrapped around his head. The four gasped when they saw a large scimitar thrust through a wide waistband wrapped around his slender rippling mid-section.

"Do you see what I see," said Chief to Worm in a whisper.

"I see it," said Worm.

"I see it too," said Shakers.

"Oh, you guys," said Royal as if chastising them. "It's a scimitar. What's the big deal?"

"Big deal," repeated Chief. "I'll tell you what the big deal is. Do you see the size of that guy? Do you see the size of sword, or scimitar or pig sticker or overgrown cheese knife or whatever it's called?" He paused and, still whispering, said: "That's what Baba told me could be used on my head if I didn't shape up."

"Oh, Baba didn't say any such thing," said Royal. "I heard every word he said to you back in the bazaar."

"I don't know what you heard, Royal, but this guy," he exclaimed pointing at himself, "heard about having his head handed to him."

Baba interrupted Chief's concerns.

"No need to worry, Master Chief, Sabu is a friend," said Baba as he indicated that the four should join him on the grassy area. "He is the Sultan's most trusted bodyguard and one of the most famous warriors in all of Baghdad."

"Sabu," repeated Chief. "Why ain't he riding an elephant?"

Baba grinned showing two rows of perfect white teeth. "Master Chief," he started still smiling, "You watch too many of those American," he paused, appeared to search for the proper word and then continued. "Movies," he stated. "You watch too many movies; too many fantasies."

"Fantasies," repeated Chief. He pivoted on his knees until his feet were off the edge of the carpet. "If this isn't a fantasy, then I must be Sinbad the Sailor."

"Be careful what you say," Baba state softly, but seriously. "We might be on the sacred ground of the Sultan's Royal Palace, but there are enemies everywhere."

"Baba, said Chief respectfully. "Why are you referring to us as, Master when you talk to us?"

"Because you are my master," replied Baba politely. "It is a term of respect."

"Really," said Chief.

Baba nodded.

Chief inched to the edge of the carpet. He took a cautious step and felt the grass on his toes. Then he put the full weight of his feet down. Standing up, he looked at his companions. "I'm not using my wish," he said cautiously. "But I think we'd be a lot better off sailing the seas with old Sinbad." He paused and looked at Worm. "You did tell me that this Sinbad the Sailor guy always escaped, didn't you?"

Will nodded.

Royal wasn't interested in what Worm and Chief had to say. She didn't waste a second. She was off the carpet and on the ground standing next to Baba. "Gee," she said sounding excited.

"Why do I feel that I've been here before?"

"Maybe it is because you have been here before, Princess," said Baba.

"Wait a minute," interrupted Chief not liking the feelings surging through him. "I just stepped off a flying carpet into this fantasy world." He seemed to get flustered. "I ain't ever been here before," he blurted out. "I ain't never seen no palm trees and flying carpets before. Heck, I ain't never been in no canoe before. Not like my ancestors."

Baba folded his arms across his chest. "You are correct, Master Chief," he said. "Your use of double negatives and the misuse of your native tongue are far from correct, but you got on the flying carpet, you flew on the carpet and you are now standing in the Royal Palace Garden of the Sultan of Baghdad." His arms unfolded and his hands came to rest on his hips. "Fantasy," he stated. "I think not."

Sabu stood firm just like a Sultan's guard should stand. His muscular arms bulged like those of professional football players and were folded across the rippled muscles of his stomach. He was not a tall man even though he was taller than they were, but he was a head taller than Baba. His dark eyes reflected the dancing flames of the torches in the garden as did his teeth that resembled perfectly shaped pearls, his mouth showing a faint glint of a warm, friendly smile. "Welcome young adventurers from a far off land to the Sultan's royal gardens," he said a slight nod of his head barely evident. He turned his massive body so it faced directly at Royal. "And, welcome home, Princess," he said. "You've been gone much too long." There was another polite nod. "Already these gardens have come alive and joy at your return."

"Welcome home," Chief repeated, his mouth open as he

stared at Royal. "You weren't kidding about that aunt of yours who was married to that Shah guy, were you?"

"Chief," said Royal carefully, softly and politely. "I've never been here before. The farthest I've even been away from home is with the Thorpe basketball team when we went to other schools. My parents have never been out of the neighborhood; not even when my father has his two weeks' vacation every summer. He thinks the Wisconsin Dells are another planet. Honest." She looked at her other friends. "Honest, guys, I have never been here before."

"I believe you, Royal," said Worm as he reached out and placed his hand on her shoulder and gave it a gentle pat.

At that moment both Baba and Sabu stiffened, Sabu's hand grasping the handle of his scimitar.

They all noticed the movement. There was no doubt in their minds. Baba and Sabu were there to protect Royal. Their friend was indeed royal, a princess; royalty to be protected even from Worm, Shakers and Chief. No harm would come to Royal. Baba and Sabu, it seemed, had pledged their lives on it.

Worm kept staring at Baba knowing he looked familiar. Then it hit him. Baba looked exactly like his favorite teacher at Thorpe School, his history teacher, Mister Toll, complete with his bushy, brown, grey streaked mustache that always needed trimming.

"Master. Worm," Baba stated, his voice showing an authority that Worm and the others now recognized as belonging to Mr. Toll when he was trying to get the attention of his students in class, "Princess Farah has returned to her home where she is to become more than, what you and your other two friends refer to her as, Royal. She has returned home by the grace of Allah to become the Sultan's new wife." He paused. "Soon, she will no longer be your friend, but your ruler. And, you three will become her loyal servants."

*****

Worm, Shakers and Chief had been ushered away from Royal. They watched her show her displeasure at being separated from them, but her kicking and trying to wrestle free from their vice like grips didn't faze Sabu or Baba.

"Why are you taking me away from my friends?" she shouted at them. "What's going to happen to them?"

Her questions about her friends being taken away seemed to fall on deaf ears. Soon, in typical Royal fashion, she was screaming at whom now appeared to be her captors; her screams were punctuated by futile attempts at slaps aimed at both Baba and Sabu. Neither of the men flinched or appeared surprised by her actions. The last words the trio heard as they stood behind the heavy wooden palace door that seemed to have a hundred more doors and an equal number of halls was, "Remember, we have three wishes!" she shouted. Then quickly adding: "Don't forget to include me."

Without their doing a thing a wooden door opened and a hand reached out and gestured for them to enter. They looked at each other and gave their all for one sign which was nothing more than a thumbs' up signal. They head the door click behind them with a loud metal clanging sound and then wished they had not been so hasty in entering the room. As they turned, each caught his breath. Standing with her back to the door was a girl who was a little older than Royal. She was every bit as pretty and had a mysterious aura about her that Worm, Chief and Shakers noticed immediately.

"Who the heck are you?" asked Chief in his usual brazen

voice. "You one of those hootchy-cootchy dancers I've seen in some of the old movie musicals on TV?"

"My name is Morgiana," said the girl. Her face was covered by a white veil from the tip of her nose down. The veil did not hide her beauty. "I am to provide you with food and to be sure that you do not go wandering off in the palace." She paused looking at each of them. "It might be dangerous for you to act foolish and try to escape away from here; even if you have your wishes."

Three sets of surprised eyes found each other.

"That grandfather of yours sure has a big mouth," said Chief to Worm, trying to hide his surprise at the girl's knowledge of their remaining wishes.

Worm gave Chief's comment a shrug.

"Are you here to be sure we don't try and escapes?" said Shakers politely. He was intrigued by the girl.

"I am here to protect you three," replied the girl.

"You're going to protect us?" asked Chief sarcastically while he slowly looked around the bare room that seemed to have what looked like three sleeping bags rolled out on a bright red tile floor. The room was barren and cold looking like nothing more than a jail cell decorated in colors of red, gold and silver. There was an oil lamp suspended by a gold chain from the ceiling of the room that appeared to be ten or more feet high. A flame flickered giving off a slight black smoke with a sweet aroma that Chief didn't recognize. "How do you plan to protect us?" he asked. "I don't see you carrying one of those overgrown cheese knives like that Sabu cat out there."

"No need," replied Morgiana with a twinkle in her eye punctuated by the flame from the lamp. "I'll just walk away," she said.

"Oh, really," said Chief feeling bold. "You're just going to walk away from the three of us," he said. Then he snapped his thumb and middle finger with a loud pop. "Just like that?" he stated.

"I could if I wanted," she said her twinkle turning into a borderline grin. Then a questioning look came to her face. She snapped her own thumb and middle finger making barely a sound. Her facial expression asked her question. "How did you that?"

"Magic," replied Chief boldly.

The girl nodded. "I have magic too," she said. Suddenly, Morgiana's index finger went to her lips.

The three boys didn't need to be told the meaning of her gesture as they watched Morgiana point at the door. She walked toward Chief almost seeming to float. Putting her mouth close to his ear she said, "Tell your friends that you're tired and want to get some sleep."

Chief nodded and did what he was told. Worm and Shakers followed his lead, Shakers letting out a loud yawn as Morgiana went to the door putting her ear against it.

"See you in the morning, guys," said Worm punctuating his remark with a yawn.

Morgiana turned and looked at the three now nervous boys. Her index finger returned to her lips for a moment. Then she gave a nod of her head indicating that there was no one outside the door standing guard and listening.

Silence returned to the room as the three boys realized that they were in trouble. Trouble meaning that their lives were in danger and that their only chance of escape rested in the hands of Morgiana who appeared to be an unwilling guard for the Sultan, Sabu and Baba. It was also Baba, they had noticed, who showed a slight sign, if only for a second, that he was concerned for the safety of the boys and Royal. Then his words and actions joined those of Sabu and they were all now prisoners not knowing what fate awaited them.

*****

The three nervous boys sat Indian style on their bed rolls with Morgiana kneeling in the middle of them. They listened in silence as their once guard turned friend whispered to them her instructions for their escape the next day.

"But, what about Royal?" asked Worm fighting to keep his voice down so no prying ears outside the door could hear what he was saying.

"She will be fine," answered Morgiana. She paused and looked serious at the three. "She will be fine provided each of you do exactly what I'm about to tell you."

Will looked at the others thinking, "The last time I did exactly what I was told is when I followed my grandfather's instructions about those stupid tooth picks."

Chief looked skeptical. "How can we trust you?" he asked. "We trusted Baba and look at what he did to us. He's no better than the palefaces who raped my people." He looked surprised at what he had just said. "You know, cheat us, steal from us, and brutalize us. You know what I mean," he continued, his anger growing and his voice beginning to rise. It stopped when Morgiana's index finger returned to her lips.

"Baba is not the enemy," she whispered. "He's protecting all of us. Again, if you do exactly what I'm about to tell you, and do it without changing one thing regardless of what you might see happening, you three and your friend the Princess will be safe from any harm." She looked very seriously at them and then stared at Chief. "No emotions from you," she warned. "Just remember the ancient adage about being sure your brain is engaged before opening your mouth or making a wrong move." Her stare continued before shifting to the others. "Do you all understand?"

Three nods were her answer.

Now here's what we are going to do tomorrow at the Sultan's wedding.

Chapter 7
Wishing on a Carpet

It was impossible for them to sleep although Shakers dozed in and out muttering, at times, to who it sounded like was his Grandma Rios. Otherwise, it was a long nervous night. When they awoke Morgiana was nowhere in sight. What they noticed immediately were three sets of clothing laid out for them; the attire being the same as what they had seen men wearing in the market place.

Chief held up a pair of what looked like baggy pants and frowned. "I ain't no Arab," he said. "My people would throw me out of both our band and tribe."

Worm was more analytical. "I think Morgiana wants us to wear this stuff over our regular clothes so we don't stand out in the crowd. She did tell us last night that we were going to the Sultan's wedding."

"Yeah," said Chief sounding angry. "We're going to get to see our buddy, Royal get married off to that roly-poly Sultan character."

"Character is right," replied Will. "He's nothing but a fat, dumpy old man." He shook his head slightly. "Royal can't marry that guy," he said. "I ain't gonna let it happen."

"She doesn't' have a choice, does she," said Shakers looking more than concerned. "I bet that mountain of rippling muscle with that razor sharp scimitar, Sabu will be guarding her like a hawk." He glanced at Worm. "And, since when did you start carrying around an atom bomb, Worm?" he asked. "Cause that's what you're gonna need when Sabu and his gang come after you."

Worm looked at his friends. "Didn't Morgiana tell us last night that she had a plan that would get all four of us out of here to safety?" He looked at each of his friends. "Did you guys hear what she said? Well, did you?"

Chief and Shakers gave a nod.

"And do you guys remember what she told us we had to do and to not change one single thing even if the situation was getting out of control and our butts were going to get burned?"

"Or get sliced off with one of those Arab meat cleavers," answered Chief with a shrug. "I'm not supposed to do a thing to save myself if that Sabu character starts swinging that overgrown cheese knife at me?" There was another shrug. "That Sabu cat carries that knife like a third arm and the darn thing is aiming at me."

"You exaggerate too much," said Worm. "Anyway, that's what Morgiana said to us last night," said Worm as he held up the outfit Morgiana left for them. "Guys, I think it's time we got dressed. We have a wedding to go to."

"Great," uttered Chief holding up his outfit. "I'm going from a Native American, an Ojibwa, to an Arab riding a flying carpet and dodging the biggest sharpest pig sticker ever created." He paused and gave a smirk to his two friends. "And, that rug isn't even an Indian blanket," he said continuing to rant on. "The medicine men back in Lac du Flambeau are gonna kick my butt for what I'm doing."

*****

They had changed into the new clothes putting them on over their jeans and t-shirts. There was plenty of room and it appeared that Morgiana had calculated what size each was and how much to allow for their street clothes. There was one thing that immediately caught each of their attention. It was their shoes. No one in Baghdad or, for that matter, in all of the Middle East, wore white running shoes. That's when they also noticed that along side of each set of clothes left for them was a pair of what resembled dark, canvas bags. Worm saw it right away. "Shoe bags," he uttered proudly. "Morgiana left these for us so we can slip them over our running shoes. Now it's for sure that no one will notice us at the wedding."

The three gave a nervous jump when they heard the large door to their room clang open. Their nerves quickly left when they saw Morgiana step in. She was carrying a large, gold tray that was piled with different fruits and nuts and slices of strange looking bread. Instead of talking to them she had kept her body partly in the doorway entrance and was talking in a language to one or more people who were congregated outside the door.

Chief thought he saw the flash of at least three blades go back and forth in the hall. All the time, Morgiana kept talking, smiling, even laughing as she positioned herself into the room, her knee pushing the door closed and inch at a time. When the door clicked shut, she turned to the three, no trace of a smile present. "Good," she said. "I see you found the clothes I left and, most important, the bags for your shoes." She set the tray on the floor in front of the three bed rolls and stepped back. "Eat, my friends," she ordered. "You're going to need your strength if we plan to get out of here alive."

"Alive," repeated Shakers nervously; "Like in the opposite of dead."

Morgiana simply nodded and seemed to float back to the

door without a sound. Her ear was pressed against the massive wooden door with what looked like huge black iron hinges. She listened intently. Then she turned and made an eating motion with both of her hands going to her mouth.

"I'm starved," said Shakers as if on cue. "I haven't eaten since yesterday and my Grandma Rios would really give me the dickens if she found out." He smiled. "She'd even give that Sabu guy the what for. She's one tough lady."

Chief had stuffed an entire wedge of bread into his mouth and was chewing as fast as he could while reaching for some dates, figs and grapes; picking up a couple of each then packing those into his mouth. "Not bad," he managed to say, his words being filtered through a full mouth.

"Yeah," said Worm. He was treating each item on the gold tray as if he were eating an individual lima bean. His taste buds were agreeing with him and he, like the others, was hungry not having eaten since the day before. Suddenly, he made a face and whatever had been in his mouth ended up in his hand. "Damn," he muttered. "The Arabs have these disgusting things here as well."

The others looked at him, Chief's jaws looking as if he were packing away extra food for their escape. Shakers ate everything on the tray even if some of the tastes didn't agree with him.

"Lima beans," said Worm, none too pleased. "I can't even go to another part of the world to get away from those things."

Chief smiled. "Try dipping a chunk of that bread into that pasty looking stuff. It's pretty good."

Worm did and what was in his mouth quickly ended up in his hand. "Chief, you're an idiot."

"Just trying to be helpful," said Chief, his puffed out cheeks unable to hide his grin.

Without them seeing her return, Morgiana was sitting on the cool, stone floor sampling from the tray. "I love figs," she said.

"My mother liked fig Newton's," said Worm. He paused, a sense of melancholy coming over him. "That's what my father told me." He glanced at Morgiana. "My mom died when I was little.

"I know," said Morgiana.

Three sets of eyes clicked after her statement.

*****

They had finished everything on the tray including the lima bean tasting things that Worm wouldn't touch. Before they realized what happened, Morgiana and the gold tray had disappeared.

"Okay, Mister Smart Ass," said Chief to Worm, "now what?"

"Hey," chimed in Shakers, "we still got three of our wishes left."

Worm took a step toward Shakers as if to grab him. "We ain't leavin' without Royal," he said his voice showing a gruff edge that said he meant business.

"Well, if she hadn't had blowin' her wish on getting us into this mess in the first place, we wouldn't have to stick out our necks so that Sabu would be coming after us with his cheese slicer," said Chief.

"Chief is right," said Shakers.

"We still ain't goin' anywhere without Royal," snapped Worm. "She's one of us and there ain't gonna be no fat, lard ass prince gonna turn her into his princess."

Shakers put up his hands as if to quell the argument. "Wait, guys," he said calmly. "We each got a wish, right?"

Worm and Chief gave a nod.

"And, Worm, didn't your grandfather say we could wish for anything?"

Worm and Chief nodded again. Worm quickly added, "Well, almost anything." He looked at his two friends. "Just as long as we didn't wish for something stupid," he said, his voice hushed as he glanced at the door.

"So, why don't one of us use his wish to get out of this place and include Royal to go with us?"

Worm's face lit up in a smile. "Right on, Brother Shakers," he said in an excited whisper, his eyes glued to the heavy door of their room that had become their cell. "I like the way you think."

Chief folded his arms across his chest and looked at his friends as if they had lost their minds. "Are you two guys looney?" he asked. "What makes you think those wishes we're supposed to have left are gonna work? What if Royal used up all that so-called magic by getting us into this mess in the first place? What if we start wishing to get out of here and nothing happens?" He looked defiantly at his two friends.

"We just can't stay locked up in this room and do nothing," said Worm.

"Well, what are you gonna do?" asked Chief. "Waste a wish on getting out of here? We don't even know where we're at in this palace and we sure don't have a clue as to where Royal is being kept. We'll end up blowing two of our wishes getting out of this fancy jail cell and then finding Royal." His eyes shifted back and forth between Worm and Shakers who were listening intently to every word. "That, my pale face friends, leaves us one wish."

"He makes sense," said Shakers. "I hate to admit it, but

"Chief is thinking logically." He broke into a grin. "That doesn't happen very often, Worm. Maybe we should listen to him."

Worm gave a frown and bit into his upper lip. Then he said: "One of my grandfather's warnings was that we shouldn't use our wishes on anything stupid like wanting all the money in the world or stuff like that. He said the wishes wouldn't work."

"Oh, brother," blurted out Chief. "Now we don't know if the wish gods are gonna save our butts or not. Remind me never to listen to you again, Worm, you wienie."

"Lighten up, Chief," said Worm, a calculating calmness in his voice. "If we word our wish carefully, I just know it will be carried out and we'll have all of us safely out of here."

Just then they heard the heavy door move. Before they could turn their heads, Morgiana was standing inside the room, her index finger to her lips.

"Wow," muttered Shakers on seeing Morgiana.

She was dressed in white silk and veils trimmed in gold. She wore gold slippers and had on gold earrings shaped in the form of loops. Similar gold shaped bracelets were on her wrists.

It was her eyes the three noticed. They were trimmed and outlined in an exotic black flecked in gold that made her look like a jungle cat.

"Wow," muttered Shakers again, only this time louder.

Chief could only make a gulping sound.

Morgiana looked at the three and gave a nod of approval. "Good," she said in a whisper. "No one will recognize you in the wedding crowd."

"Wedding crowd?" asked Worm feeling his need growing to save Royal. "Royal's gonna marry that rich, fat guy? I don't think so. Not if I can help it."

"You can't," whispered Morgiana. "But, I can." She turned and was back at the door appearing not to have moved a muscle. A quick glance in each direction down the hall had her showing she was pleased. "The guards are gone, but they'll be back when they realize I sent them on what you from the west call a wild goose chase."

The three looked at one another and, before they could say a word, Morgiana said to them: "Come. It is time." She gave them a serious look that scared each of them. "Remember, if you value your lives and the life of your friend, do exactly as I instruct."

Chapter 8
Open Sesame

Morgiana led them through a maze of narrow, dark halls, the ceilings so low that they had to walk stooped over. Chief didn't like the idea of holding hands, especially Shakers, but those were Morgiana's instructions and Chief knew she meant business.

Worm held the hand of Shakers while clutching onto Morgiana's tiny hand. Actually, it was the other way around. Morgiana all but squeezed the life out of Worm's fingers. He had never felt a grip so tight; not even from his Uncle Cas who was known as Uncle Casbah using the name of his tavern as his nickname. Uncle Cas had once been a professional wrestler, but Worm felt that Morgiana could crush him with her grip.

The hall passageways had turned so black the three friends were glad they were holding on to one another. One would stumble in the dark and his friend would increase the pressure on their hands and pull him along until balance was regained. They made what seemed like a hair pin turn and that's when they saw a sliver of light at the end of what seemed to them to be a tunnel.

Morgiana stopped suddenly.

Worm could feel her slowly pull him along; the others staying close behind; so close that Chief was stepping on Shakers and Shakers was stepping on Worm's ankles and toes.

Morgiana stopped. She was just on the edge of the faint light into the tunnel. Her head slowly inched forward until one eye was peering through the slit in the wall. "Very good," she muttered.

Worm heard her. Chief and Shakers did not.

Morgiana reached up with her free hand and grabbed Worm by the neck.

Worm was surprised at how strong her hand gripped him.

Morgiana slowly pulled him down so that his ear was even with her mouth. "The coast is clear," she said to him. "Tell the others." Her grip on his neck seemed to tighten. "Quietly," she warned. "And tell them not to move or say a word until I give the signal."

Worm did what he was told.

No one moved a muscle. No one blinked. It was as if each of the three friends had stopped breathing. The only sound they heard was that of their hearts beating; if they could have muffled that they would have.

They waited for what seemed like an hour. Then Morgiana said: "Follow me and keep your heads down. Don't stop for anything."

They obeyed their mysterious guide and followed her through the slit in the wall as if it were a curtain opening for them. Chief was the last one through and he had to check the slit with his own hand. He was shocked to find that it was solid, but he didn't have time to examine it more closely since Morgiana was pulling them along.

They discovered they were in a vast garden that was decorated for some kind of gala celebration. It was. The celebration was a wedding.

Morgiana kept pulling them along. She led them on a winding path that followed the perimeter of the garden. The lush, green garden was ringed by a vine covered wall that stood over twenty feet tall. Festive tents lined the path they followed. There were the sounds of strange music and songs very foreign to them; even the aromas of food cooking; smells and odors new to them. Ahead of them loomed a giant wooden gate. Each of them recognized it instantly. It was the gate they had flown over on the flying carpet with Baba and, now, looking up at it, each of them knew there was no way they could get out from behind the formidable walls without help. Each of them prayed that Morgiana was that help.

Morgiana slowed her pace and began to follow a course that seemed to weave in between the tents. Each tent had spires of colorful flowers on pedestals standing like sentries guarding the pathway.

The three friends found themselves in awe, spellbound by the opulence surrounding them. Their combined awes quickly vanished when they saw Sabu. He was standing talking to Baba. Each man was decked out in wedding finery; blinding white clothing trimmed in gold with rubies, emeralds, pearls and diamonds adorning the wide waist bands they wore. Sabu's muscles bulged through a red velvet vest he wore. Baba was covered by a white shirt with a red bejeweled vest open in front. There were no signs of his muscles.

"Oh, crap," said Worm when he spotted the two men.

"Double crap," said Shakers. His grip on the hands of his two friends was total strangulation.

Chief didn't say a word, but the look on his face concerned the others. The look was obvious: *I'm gonna use my wish whether you two bozos like it or not.*

Before any wish could be made, they felt Morgiana gently lead them behind the last of the tents before the gate.

Worm saw it first and felt numb. Shakers also felt the same. Chief simply said, "I'll be dipped in Bambi poop."

Lying on the ground behind the tent out of sight from any of the hundreds of thousands of guests and well-wishers attending the wedding was a rolled-up carpet. They recognized it immediately and then felt a sense of worry creep over them.

"Baba's the only guy who knows how to fly that thing," said Chief. He kicked at the ground in disgust. "Double Bambi poop," he muttered.

"Maybe Morgiana knows how to fly that carpet," said Shakers. "Ain't she some kind of Arab or something like that?"

"Right," said Chief, then making another clicking sound with his middle finger and thumb. Hey, Worm," he said. "Didn't you tell me you read about her knocking off those forty thieves in the Arabian Nights book you read."

"I did," said Worm. "But, I don't know if she's the same Morgiana." Worm gave a gentle tug on Morgiana's hand. "Are you?"

He never got the chance to hear her answer.

"No need," she said. "Our friend, Baba will do it."

If their vocal chords didn't freeze in their throats, they all would've repeated the old Arab's name in a shouted one-word question.

"BABA?!?!"

*****

The three friends barely caught their breath when they saw Morgiana let go of Worm's hand and make her way around the tent to the other side. It wasn't that she had walked to the other side. She was doing a slow, seductive dance, her feet barely touching the tips of the well-manicured green grass, her golden bracelets giving off a musical beat.

Worm, Shakers and Chief stood like three pedestals without

vases or flowers.

Morgiana had been gone only a few moments before she reappeared. She was holding someone's hand and there was uproarious laughter coming from the other side of the tent.

Worm, Shakers and Chief didn't feel like laughing when they saw who belonged to hand Morgiana was holding. It was Baba's.

"Bambi, you ain't got enough poop to help us in this case," said Chief as he tried to figure out what his wish would say. He knew he had to include Royal and wanted to phrase his plea so that the four of them would be saved.

Chief's thoughts were interrupted by the loud sound of drums and horns blaring. To Chief and the others, it sounded like thousands of drums and horns. It was. As he hastily formulated his wish, Chief saw Baba unroll the carpet. It was if he had only taken a second to accomplish the task. Before them was the carpet, the same one that had brought them over the wall with several claps of Baba's hands and as many grunts.

Baba did not smile. Morgiana did not smile. Baba clapped his hands and the carpet lifted off the ground like before, just high enough for the passengers to get on. Without a single word, they all took a step up and got on the carpet.

Morgiana signaled that the three boys should lie down on their stomachs. "You are not to show yourselves," she warned. "The slightest glimpse of any one of you will set off alarms like you've never known. And with those alarms will bring pain that you never knew existed." She paused looking down at the three friends who were trying to look at her from their prone positions, their heads twisted around. "Sabu will administer that pain."

Three faces pressed into the carpet.

There was the grunt from Baba that they recognized and the

clap of his hands. They could feel the carpet rise.

"We are part of the wedding ceremony festivities," they heard Morgiana say. They couldn't see her smiling and waving at the crowd below who had just started to look up. Baba's magic is in great demand," she said without losing her smile and her energetic waving and dancing. "The Sultan has so commanded."

Baba was waving as if he were the guest of honor riding a float in a high school homecoming parade. The three prone passengers didn't dare look. They did, however, hear another grunt from Baba and several more hand claps.

The drums continued to explode along with the blare from the horns. The crowd was growing excited and all Worm could do was think about Royal. He didn't dare say a word even though his thoughts were on the brink of exploding from him. *If only I could help her; get her out of here and make her safe.*

Baba had the magic carpet hovering above the crowd and steering it slowly to a position that would be behind and just above the heads of the wedding party; a giant wedding canopy with five passengers aboard waited for the wedding ceremony to begin. Baba was also waiting, but not for long.

Morgiana kept up her waving. Her gyrating dance steps were stationary, but Will, Chief and Shakers feared that if she gyrated any harder, any faster, she would dance herself off the carpet.

The crowd's attention suddenly focused on the soon-to-be new princess. Even Morgiana lost her calm and almost missed a dance step and a wave at what she saw. Royal was more than beautiful. She was adorned in the finest of eastern silks; all white and trimmed in real gold. Her golden slippers glistened in the sunlight. So, did her eyes that were outlined in black giving her a cat like appearance; the black outlined in gold. A white veil covered the lower half of her face from just below her eyes. The crowd went silent as the short, rotund Sultan looking like a giant golden nugget stepped proudly beside his about to be new bride.

Baba had waited for this moment. It was the only time he knew that not a soul in the palace would be on guard, alert for danger of any kind. What no one in the crowd expected was that a wedding canopy in the form of a flying carpet with two trusted servants aboard would drop from the sky, lift the about-to-be-princes aboard and be over the palace wall heading toward the surrounding mountains.

Worm, Chief and Shakers heard Baba's clap and commands. The claps were different from the ones they had heard before; the shouted orders meaningless to them because of the language difference. What surprised them were Morgiana's orders. They were more than orders; they were shouts and those shouts were directed to each of them; each having a specific task.

As the magic carpet dipped low and raced forward, Morgiana called out Royal's name. At the same time, Worm, Chief and Shakers were on their knees at the edge of the carpet. Chief and Shakers had their hands and arms extended, reaching for Royal. Worm had latched on to their ankles.

Royal put her athletic skills as a basketball player into use instantly. Her hands went up; she leaped and caught the extended hands of Chief and Shakers. There was a hard yank and she was on the carpet being forced face down by Worm. The moment she hit the carpet he had let go of the ankles of his two friends and had pulled out what looked like a small blanket the color of Baba's carpet. He quickly covered Royal with it according to Morgiana's instructions. The bride-to-be was out of sight and Baba sent the carpet soaring for altitude while trying to get as much speed from the flying carpet as his claps and commands could muster.

More commands echoed from Baba as did the clapping of his hands. The magic carpet seemed to jump and began to rise up so fast and high that the passengers feared that they might be blown off. They felt themselves being forced down because of the immense pressure.

At first everyone in the crowd watched in a silent awe. No one made a sound. Then applause and cheers broke out. This, indeed, had to be part of the ceremonial festivities. Sabu put an end to any ill-timed merriment with a shout and a raised scimitar that even the four infidels on the carpet recognized with or without a language barrier. What appeared to be several arrow-like projectiles whizzed under the carpet, the carpet too high to be in danger. There was another cry from a very angry Sabu. A horde of mounted warriors on jet black stallions appeared from out of nowhere and galloped towards the gates of the palace that seemed to be opening so fast they appeared to be made of leftover golden silk from the wedding attire of the bride to be.

A scared, but angry Royal pushed her way out from under the blanket and the force of Worm's arms pinning her down. "What happened?' she asked sounding out of breath.

"You're safe," said Morgiana, her voice sounding comforting.

"At least for now," said Baba without looking at the passengers, his eyes fixed on the horizon and a vast valley that was ahead. "Danger is only for the complacent," he said then turning his attention back to the valley entrance. He took a quick glance back and could see the clack outline of the stallions and the clouds of dust they were sending up. They were heading in the same direction Baba was guiding his carpet.

Baba smiled knowing that he would reach the same valley that the one hundred riders and their stallions were heading. "So beautiful a beast," he muttered. "So brutal the riders." His eyes turned sad. "May Allah look favorably upon us."

Worm put his arms around Royal's shoulders and gently pulled her close for safety; her black and gold eye liner being smeared and staining the tunic he wore. She pulled away from Worm and found it strange that he was laughing. "What's so funny?" she shouted at him. "Do you think my having to get married to that fat, old man is funny?" she barked at him. "Well, do you?"

Worm's head went from side to side a couple of times before he said, "No, I don't think you're getting married to that fat, old man if funny." His laughter had turned to a grin. "But, your eyes making you look like a raccoon on drugs is hysterical." He continued to grin. "What's even funnier is what your parents would say if they saw you looking like you hadn't washed your face in a year."

Royal rubbed at the make-up around her eyes with her fists trying to rub the eye liner off by beating it into submission. She took a quick look around the carpet and then leaned to the edge and glanced down. There was the sound of a gulp from her. "Worm, what happened back there?"

Worm stopped laughing and gave her a sympathetic look. "I really don't know," he said softly. "You'll have to ask Morgiana and Baba. They're the ones who got you out of that awful mess back there." He paused and his head went from side-to-side once. "And the four of us better thank them both for getting us out of that palace and away from that awful Sultan and that crazed killer, Sabu."

"Awful sultan, heck," said Chief. He was still kneeling at the edge of the carpet alongside Shakers, the two of them not moving after they had lifted Royal aboard. "That sultan guy was a big sissy; a fat little mama's boy," he said, his cockiness returning. Then his cockiness vanished when he said: "That Sabu guy looked like he wanted to slice us up and serve us to the wedding guests. "Yeah, Worm, you're right. Only we all should be thanking Morgiana and Baba."

"You may give your thanks to Allah when we are indeed safe," said Baba as he gave a subtle command to the carpet that had entered the opening to a large picturesque valley that, to the untrained eye, was well fortified on all sides. The carpet zoomed into the valley perfectly without a clap or a grunt from Baba. In moments, the carpet made another sharp right turn entering the opening to another valley.

"We will all be thankful when we're out of reach of the Sultan's warriors," said Morgiana, her eyes trained on the floor of the second valley instead of on the four passengers.

Baba suddenly unleashed several more commands. Those were followed by several staccato claps and the magic carpet responded smoothly with another sharp turn, this one to the left. Several seconds later the carpet banked to the right, shot up quickly to avoid a collision with a large outcropping of rock then began to slow down. Baba appeared to be searching for something. What they didn't know, that is, except for Shakers, was what Baba was looking for.

Shakers scooted next to Baba who stood like a captain at the helm of his ship and politely asked: "Do I get to say, Open Sesame?"

Baba gave a wry smile.

Chapter 9
"Sailing, Sailing…."

Shakers had a feeling that Baba and Morgiana were going to head for the safety of a cave he had read about long before Worm had been given the Arabian Nights book with the story of Ali Baba and the Forty Thieves. His memory was crystal clear of the author's description of the cave, its whereabouts and the surrounding mountainous terrain.

"Mister Baba," said Shakers speaking for the first time without tension and fear since Morgiana had ordered the three to lie face down on the carpet and not say a word. "Mister Baba," he repeated politely, "you're taking us to Ali Baba's cave, aren't you?"

"You are, indeed, the son of two university professors," replied Baba as he continued to skillfully navigate the treacherous area that could have all of their bodies scattered over the rocks below. "We are heading to the cave albeit only for a temporary visit."

"Temporary?' asked Shakers, his curiosity continuing to grow along with accompany feelings of excitement and being scarred.

"We need to prepare ourselves for the arduous journey ahead; a journey that will take you and your friends to safety and return you to your home called Chicago," he said, his eyes fixed on an area where he intended to land the carpet. "This new journey will also return Morgiana and I to our home."

"You'll be leaving us?" asked Shakers. "You and Morgiana?"
Baba nodded.

"But where will you take us?" Shakers asked. "How do we get to Chicago from here?" He paused. "I don't think our three wishes are enough."

"Fear not, young Master Shakers," said Baba. "If all goes according to plan, you will be safe with your grandmother," he continued then pausing. "Grandma River I believe you refer to the lady who provides for all of your worldly needs."

Shakers now nodded back at Baba.

The magic carpet did a series of left and right turns and began to descend.

"Hey," Chief called out. "Why are we getting lower? This big pile of thread isn't going to crash, is it?"

Baba seemed to ignore Chief's question as he steered the carpet at a higher rate of speed only inches off the ground. There were multiple series of quick up and down movements as the carpet avoided larger rocks and boulders, barely clearing each one. All the while Baba kept muttering commands to the carpet.

Then they all noticed it at once.

"Geez," muttered Worm.

"Holy cow," said Chief, his remark louder than Worm's.

"Oh, my," said Royal who had spent almost the entire trip conversing with Morgiana.

"I was right," exclaimed Shakers.

"You were indeed, Master Shakers," said Baba as the carpet stopped and settled gently to the ground in front of an immense boulder that looked like a giant gate guarding the entrance to a massive opening in the side of a mountain. "Would you like to do the honors?"

Shakers almost jumped out of his skin. Then, in the next instant, he let out a shout that startled his friends. "Open Sesame!"

The four friends felt and heard the ground begin to vibrate and rumble. Clouds of dust began to show along the outline of the giant boulder. Clusters of small pebbles and stones rolled out of the growing outline of the boulder.

"It's moving," said Worm to his friends who could see the obvious.

"Shakers," said Chief in his usual sarcastic voice, "what has your big mouth gotten us into?"

"Oh, my, gosh," Royal managed to say as she held on to Worm's arm.

The vibrating and rumble of the boulder moving continued as the huge stone opened like a giant gate, its hinges appearing to be crusted with years of rust.

"It's real," said Shakers in awe. "Ali Baba's cave is for real." Then he exclaimed loudly so that his one word echoed throughout the valley. "WOW!"

Morgiana was now at Baba's side, the two of them having stepped off the carpet. Baba started for the opening into the cave and Morgiana turned to the four friends and said, "Come. There is no time to waste," she said without breaking her stride as she followed Baba. The Sultan's assassins on black horses will be here shortly."

"But those guys with the big cheese knives are on horses," said Chief. "They ain't gonna get through these mountains for at least a week."

"Those horses are like our magic carpet," said Morgiana as she waved for the four friends to hurry up. "Your week, Mister Chief, will be less than hour for them." She continued to wave to them to catch up. "Hurry," she ordered. "We have not time to waste."

*****

The musketeers stood in the vast cave their eyes unable to keep up with everything they saw and wanted to see. The inside of the cave seemed to go on forever in all directions. There didn't seem to be a ceiling. All they saw was darkness. The light streaming into the cave through the opening reflected off mounds and piles of gold and jewels. There were weapons made of gold; there were mounds of household items such as plates and platters, cup and goblets, even chalices. Figurines and sculptures resembling anything that once lived or had been created or worshipped were piled on top of each other in haphazard mounds, some so high the four couldn't climb over in the hour they had left. That hour, however, had now been cut in half.

Baba suddenly appeared from out of the dark in front of them. Then Morgiana appeared. They both were waving at the friends to join them. "Hurry," called out Morgiana. "Time is of the essence."

"Bring your muscles as well," said Baba, his voice showing an increased sense of urgency for the first time since they had met him.

They were surprised that they had no trouble following Baba and Morgiana in the dark. They both appeared to be casting off a halo of light. In moments, they were standing in front of what looked like neatly aligned rows and aisles of bags. Each was labeled in a language they could not read.

Morgiana motioned to Royal. "Come, Princess," she said respectfully. "You will carry these two bags." She pointed. "They're not too heavy, but they have extra garments we need for where we're going."

Royal didn't ask and began to follow Morgiana who was carrying four similar bags, two in each hand.

Worm, Chief and Shakers watched as Royal followed Morgiana from the black of the cave; a halo of light coming from Morgiana's silhouette. All three almost jumped out of their skins when they heard Baba's loud clap and what sounded like an admonishment to them.

"By the grace of Allah's beard," shouted Baba, a red fire seeming to come from his eyes; the fire lighting up the cave. "You are lazier than a trio of goats with full stomachs." He pointed at a pile of sacks that were similar in the size and shape that Royal and Morgiana had carried by them. "Four each," he ordered again. "And, if you three demented jackals with no signs of intelligence value those worthless hides of yours, you'll be on our carpet before the women."

Chief then made the biggest mistake of his life by asking: "What's in the bags?"

A thundering roar echoed from Baba's throat. That was followed by tongues of flame leaping from his eyes. His index finger pointed in the direction they were to go only this time his finger had turned into the shape of a black serpent.

Before Royal and Morgiana realized, Worm, Chief and Shakers had caught up to them. Without saying a word, they continued at a full sprint, each carrying eight bags, heading for the opening to the cave and the safety of the magic carpet.

Out of breath, their hearts pounding and arms aching, they dropped to their knees on the carpet. "I ain't likin' this one bit," gasped Chief, his hands and arms thanking him for taking the load away from them. "That Baba is one strange stud."

"I think he's just trying to protect us," said Worm, his chest still heaving and his hands and arms sending him the same message that Chief's was sending to him. "I read that in the Arabian Nights book my grandpa gave me."

"Did you read about some crazy old dude turning into a boa constrictor?" asked Chief. "I think not, pal. No way, Jose."

"It was an illusion," added Shakers. "Some of these Arab guys know how to hypnotize and do magic stuff like that. I read that too. Just like Worm did."

Just then Morgiana and Royal joined the three on the carpet. "Were you three guys getting in shape to go out for Thorpe's track team?" asked Royal. She smiled at them. "Oh, I forgot, Thorpe doesn't have a track team."

"No track team," said Worm, his breathing no longer punctuated with gasps for air. "Baba told us to hurry and we were hurrying."

"Yeah," said Chief. "More like running for our lives."

"Baba said we didn't have any time to waste," said Shakers as he saw Baba emerge from the cave. He was carrying what looked like a golden staff in one hand and a single bag, like the others, in his opposite hand. "Are you ready?" he asked the group.

"No!" shouted Chief. He jumped off the carpet and sprinted back toward the cave.

The others looked at one another in shock. Then the shock turned to concern as they heard a faint rumbling sound.

"The black stallions," said Baba. "They're here faster than I thought." He motioned to the others to secure the bags in the middle of the carpet. "Hurry," he ordered. "We don't have a moment to spare."

"But what about, Chief?" asked Shakers, his eyes focused on the entrance to the cave.

"We're not leaving our friend," said Worm. "No way. It's one for all and all for one."

"If we wait, you'll be able to spend eternity with your friend in what you infidels refer to as Heaven." He pursed his lips for a moment and then softly said, "Perhaps what you call Hell."

"Please, Baba," said Royal reaching out and touching his arm. Her eyes were pleading.

"Your friend will find a way to us," he said. Then there was the clap of his hands and garbled commands and the carpet became airborne; this time the thrust was up and over the mouth of the cave almost causing Shakers to lose his balance and fall off the carpet.

Worm's hands shot out and he grabbed Shaker by the knees in a bear hug. With a twist, turn and the pressure of a football player making a tackle, he had Shakers on his back topping off the stowed bags from the cave.

About that time the world seemed to go insane. Arrows whizzed over their heads; a few sticking in the bags where Shakers was sprawled. Some of the arrows hit the carpet; the carpet flinching and bucking as if it had been injured and was showing pain. Below, Chief had sprinted out of the cave with something in his hand. Then two things made him turn and head back to the entrance. The first was that there was no magic carpet waiting for him. That was a big cause of concern for him. His concern for a magic carpet was swept aside by the sight of what appeared to be a hundred black stallions with smoke snorting from their nostrils. At that point, Chief knew he was in trouble. Mounted on each of the horses was a warrior carrying a golden lance with the longest, sharpest blade he had ever seen. Then he really got scared. Each warrior wore a scimitar; these appearing to be bigger and sharper than the one carried by Sabu. "Oh, crap," he said, as his head and eyes shifted back and forth almost in a frenzy. His mind whirled, the options for escape and saving his life being generated so fast he couldn't get his hands around any of them. The only thing he hung to was the souvenir he had taken from the cave. It was a golden lamp.

When they were all in the cave earlier following Baba he had seen the lamp and just knew it possessed magic; perhaps even containing a genie. He had to have it.

Now, facing almost certain annihilation, he pleaded with the golden lamp to save him. He pleaded and begged shouting command after command but no help came. The horses were now pawing at the earth and grins were beginning to form on the faces of their riders.

"Oh, crap," he muttered again. "Should I close the cave and lock myself in. I'll be safe. I can hide. Maybe those guys will never find me in the dark.

All one hundred riders seemed to dismount from the black stallions as if in a well-orchestrated, precision show of military discipline and might. In another well-orchestrated move, their scimitars were removed, their golden blades reflecting the sun and almost blinding their prey.

"Oh, crap," said Chief. He wanted to turn and run but knew that choice would be useless. "Oh, crap," he said again a sigh escaping him. Then he said, "Sorry, Worm." He used his wish.

*****

Baba had steered the magic carpet and its four passengers and cargo away from danger. With everyone temporarily safe he began to carefully remove the arrows that had been imbedded in the carpet. Only Morgiana understood his words that seemed to be coated with sympathy and understanding. As he removed the last arrow, tossing it over the side to the rocky canyon floor below, they all felt a jolt as if the carpet had collided with a heavy object. It had.

Kneeling on the carpet in front of them was Chief; his lantern clutched to his chest.

Chief's three friends looked at him in amazement, happy to see him safe after coming face-to-face with death.

"Oh, thank God you're safe," said "Royal carefully inching her way across the crowded carpet. She put her arms around him and gave him a hug.

"Wow, Chief," said Shakers feeling his eyes welling up with tears. "You made it, man. Now I really believe in those Ojibwa medicine men you brag about."

Worm gave Chief a playful punch in his upper arm, smiled and said, "You used it, didn't you?"

Chief's head went up and down once. "Yeah," he said sounding apologetic. "I had to. Nothing else worked."

Baba looked concerned. "Did you order the cave closed?"

Chief's eyes were downcast. "I didn't know how," he said quietly. "I was scared. I tried everything. Nothing worked. I was even going to go back where you took us, Baba and hide." Then Chief did something he had never done in front of any of his friends before. He started to cry.

It was Baba who surprisingly put his hand on Chief's shoulder to comfort him. "Hiding was a good choice, Master Chief, if you closed the opening to the cave sooner." said Baba. He surprised everyone by clapping his hands several times and muttering a few words in Arabic. The magic carpet went into a slow vertical climb until everyone on board could see the black stallions and the hundred palace warriors standing by their mounts.

"You would've been safe if you had acted sooner, Master Chief," he said. "Let me show you."

The four friends watched the scene below. They could see some of the warriors leading their horses toward the opening of the cave. They could also see that Baba appeared to be calculating, waiting for the right moment. They didn't wait long. Surprising his passenger and even the warriors well below them, he shouted at the top of his voice, "Close, Sesame!"

They watched the giant boulder in front of the opening start to close. Horses and warriors were losing the rigid military discipline they had exhibited so far. Both animal and man began to panic as the roar of the giant boulder door continued to close. Joining the roar was a sound from above the cave.

"Oh, my, God," muttered Royal as she latched on to Worm's arm.

"I ain't never seen one of those before," said Chief. "My people have used rock slides, but not by moving an entire mountain."

"Wow," said Shaker unable to take his eyes off of the scene below.

"That's ain't no avalanche," said Worm, his arm around Royal and pulling her close to him. "It's the world coming to an end."

"Only an end to evil," said Baba as Morgiana stood beside him. "You did well last night," he said to Morgiana admiringly. "Even better than when you filled those giant jars with hot oil to rid the world of the notorious forty thieves."

"I take no credit," said Morgiana. "As you said, Baba," she continued, "evil needed to come to an end."

The four-young people were having a difficult time understanding what they were seeing on the canyon floor directly below them. Horses were stampeding but had no place to run. The entrance and exit to the cave were one in the same and mountains of newly fallen rocks blocked the way. As the giant boulder door closed with a rumble and a thud, several warriors, thinking they had some mysterious powers granted to them by the Sultan, were crushed in the seam of the door. While this was going on everyone in the valley could now hear another sound, a growing rumble that was greater than the sounds they had just heard by a hundred-fold. Even up on the magic carpet the sound was so deafening that is forced hands to ears. Wide eyes couldn't believe what happened next. The mountains on all sides started to crumble. Small stones rolled down steep sides and began to spill onto the warriors and their horses causing an annoyance at best and making the warriors angry. Their anger vanished as the pebbles and stone turned to rocks. Then the rocks turned to boulders and the boulders to slabs of jagged stone. Scimitars swatted, lances jabbed and shields were thrust above heads. They were no match for what rained down upon them. Horses and their once proud riders cried out. The cries didn't last long turning into whimpers and then silence.

They all watched until the dust settled. There were no signs of life. There were also no sign that a cave filled with treasures ever existed.

"What do we do now, Baba?" asked Worm, his arm still around Royal's shoulder.

Baba shifted back to his position on the magic carpet that he assumed when steering the craft. "Remember all of those bags I had all of you carry out of the cave?" he asked.

They all glanced at the pile of bags they had stowed in the center of the carpet.

"What about them?" asked Chief, the swagger back in his voice.

"Supplies," said Baba calmly. He looked at each of his passengers. "We're going on a trip," he said. "A long, long trip."

"But why?" asked Royal.

"You want to get home, don't you," answered Baba

"Ah, yeah, man," replied Chief. "We all do."

"Yes, Master Chief, we all do," said Baba. He glanced at Morgiana. "Especially this brave eradicator of evil and yours truly," he said"

"Baba, sir," said Worm, "When does this long, long trip begin and where does it start?"

"It has already begun," said Baba. He muttered a few commands to the magic carpet and they began to gain altitude and fly straight ahead. "Now I suggest you all start unpacking those bags and sort out the supplies. We're going to need every last item in those bags for where we are going."

"Where are we going, Baba, sir?" asked Worm, his curiosity about to leap out of him.

For a rare time, Baba smiled. "We're going sailing with a friend of mine."

"Sailing?" repeated Worm.

Shakers leaped up from where he was kneeling opening several bags. "We're sailing with Sinbad the Sailor," he shouted with glee. "I just know its Sinbad. It is him, isn't it Baba? We're going sailing with Sinbad the Sailor."

Baba smiled.

Part II
The Voyage Home

Chapter 10
On Air, Land and Sinbad

What Worm and his three friends thought would be a long journey on the magic flying carpet wasn't. Baba clapped his hands several different times and gave commands to the rug like they had seen and heard before. The carpet obeyed and they watched the treacherous mountains below slowly lose their menacing shapes and slowly transform into lush green hills filled with trees none of them they had ever seen before in their home of Chicago. None of them had said a word as the trip continued; each staying put in the exact place they had been when Chief had joined them after using his wish.

It was Shakers who spoke first by asking Baba: "Are we really going to meet Sinbad the Sailor?"

Baba's turbaned head went up and down once; his attention focused on the direction the carpet was headed.

"Wow," said Shakers, his enthusiasm spilling out. "I just hope we don't meet any of those monsters Sinbad did if he's going to sail us home."

"Fear not, Mister Shakers," said Baba still concentrating on where the carpet was headed. "Sinbad's days filled with arduous adventure have passed him by. His days are spent enjoying the harvested fruits of his seven voyages."

"I read about some of Sinbad's voyages," chimed in Worm. "They were in a book my grandfather gave me."

Baba nodded and said, "I know."

"You do?" repeated Worm.

Baba nodded again. "A Thousand and One Nights, isn't that so, Master Worm?"

"Yeah, Mister Baba, but…."

"Seven very adventurous and dangerous voyages," said Baba. He glanced at Worm. "In no particular order, I believe Sinbad was on an island with cannibals."

"Cannibals?" said Chief interrupting Baba. "You mean those guys who prefer to eat other guys and not eat at Taco Bell?"

"Of this Taco Bell I know not," said Baba. "But, yes, Mister Chief, cannibals eat other humans." He gave a serious look at Chief and then glanced at the others. "Sinbad also encountered giant snakes that were so big and powerful they could crush an elephant or a rhinoceros and ingest them whole."

"As in swallow?" asked Shakers timidly. "

"That is so, Master Shakers," answered Baba.

Then Worm, remembering what he had read about Sinbad's voyages asked: "Did Sinbad really discover a valley filled with diamonds, Mister Baba?"

"That is so," answered Baba. "Diamonds so big some were the size of melons. One diamond like that for each of you and you would be wealthy beyond your wildest dreams."

"But, Mister Baba," Worm continued; "didn't Sinbad have to defend himself from those giant birds that dropped large boulders on his ship and sank it? Kind of like the boulders back at the cave that took care of the Sultan's army and those black stallions."

Baba nodded. "It is so."

"Hey," Chief blurted out, "does this Sinbad guy get his kicks fighting with monsters? Geez, now I'm kind of sorry I used up my wish. I'm not feeling so hot about meeting this guy." Chief shifted his weight from his knees to sitting cross legged. Nervous curiosity had him reaching for one of the sacks they had carried from the cave and began to open it. Stopping, as if by some silent command, he asked: "Baba what's in all of these bags you made us haul out of that old Sesame place?"

"The essentials for life," Master Chief," said Baba. He turned his attention to his young questioner. "Food, clothing and shelter," he continued. "The same as your native people would take when they moved to, how shall I say, more hospital surroundings. As we are now doing."

"Hospitable as in safe," replied Chief. "Like in being back home? Like in not having to worry about getting eaten alive?"

Thou tends to exaggerate, Master Chief," said Baba, his attention shifting back to the direction they were headed.

"Baba," said Chief his hands coming away from the sack he was opening, "you remind me of one of my teachers at Thorpe School. "You're kind of cool like him. You're a good guy; a bit tough and a bit on the weird side, but you're cool."

"Have I been blessed with a compliment, Mister Chief?" asked Baba. "Or, is this cool condition you mention a positive or negative?"

"Cool's definitely good, Baba," said Chief with a smile. "Our teacher, Mister Toll, is very cool. Has a mustache almost like yours, but not as big. All us kids tease him and ask him if he's trying to attract girls with his mustache."

"I see," said Baba not looking back; a broad grin hidden from his passengers. "Ahhhhh," he muttered. "We are here."

"We are?" asked Royal leaning forward and trying to see what was ahead of them.

"Where's here?" asked Shakers. He was on all fours his head over the end of the carpet looking down.

"There," said Baba without giving any indication to the direction of their destination.

"I don't see anything," said Shakers leaning forward even more.

"Where's there?" asked Worm as he and Royal inched closer to the edge until they were next to Shakers. "We don't see anything but those things that look like palm trees."

"Very good observation, Mister Worm," said Baba. "Did you study the science of biology with this cool teacher, Mister Toll."

"Holy crap," said Chief as he stood straight up so fast he looked like he popped out of Jack in the Box. "I see it, Baba," he stated unable to hide his excitement. "There's a boat tied up down there," he said almost in a shout. "A big boat!" He looked at Baba who looked back at him. "That's Sinbad's boat, isn't it?"

"Mister Chief," said Baba now showing his smile to his passengers. "Your powers of deductive reasoning amaze even Allah."

Wow," they all heard Shakers state. "I see it too." He leaned forward. "Wow," he said again. "That boat's hidden in a harbor. I see what looks like a narrow river that leads out of that jungle of trees down there. Wow, it leads to what looks like an ocean. An ocean that's going to get us home." He let out a cry as both of his hands slid off the front of the carpet and he felt himself drop forward. Then he felt several sets of hands grabbing at his ankles and legs and dragging him back.

*****

They had watched in amazement how Baba directed the flying carpet out over what Shakers had described as an ocean and then back following the course of the almost hidden river.

Before they knew it, the carpet had settled down on a lush plot of soft grass the color of sparkling emeralds. The color was apropos since real emeralds were embedded in the grass and spread out in all directions.

Looking around at their new surroundings they were startled by a friendly voice that shouted out, "Welcome aboard you land lubbers!" The welcome was followed by a loud raucous laugh. "And welcome to you too, Baba, you old camel driver, you."

The man who greeted them wasted no time and jumped up on the carpet and through his arms around Baba giving him a big hug. "You even still smell like a camel," he said loudly. "Maybe throw in a goat or two, Baba. "You've spent too many nights impressing that Sultan of yours by bringing caravans loaded with ill gotten goods into his palace of evil.

Baba wrapped his arms around the man and said, "Sinbad, a giant, man eating cannibal, birds that can carry an elephant and snakes that can eat both the giant bird and the elephant being carried in one bite haven't changed your sense of humor." He pulled away from Sinbad and both of them looked at each other, grinned and then broke into loud laughter.

The four-young people had no clue as to what was going on before their eyes. Morgiana did. She gave a nod to Royal who instantly knew what to do. Grabbing a sack in each hand she started to one end of the carpet and set her two bags down on the emerald grass along side of the bags Morgiana had set down. Worm, Shakers and Chief each grabbed four of the bags—two in each hand—and hauled what Baba had early described as the necessities of life and placed them in a pile with the others.

"Ah, Baba," said Sinbad still looking and sounding jovial. "I see you've brought me a well disciplined crew. Kind of scrawny looking lot, but I think they'll handle my ship well." He paused and winked at Baba. "Sailing to this place called Chicago, huh?" he asked his broad grin now gone replaced by two rows of pearl white teeth. "Only thing I ever heard about that place is it has a name that means, smelly onions." He wrinkled his nose. "I hope not too smelly," he continued. "I'm thinking of raking up these emeralds and trying to sell them there. Do you think their rulers might be interested in making a deal for precious gems with this here old sea dog?" A loud roar of a laugh echoed from his throat.

"He's kind of handsome," said Royal to Morgiana.

"That he is," Morgiana whispered back. "Many a maiden has set her designs on him and his fortunes I've heard." She continued to talk to Royal in a whisper and then paused to look and see if Baba and Sinbad were listening. "None have succeeded."

"He has the bluest eyes I have ever seen," whispered Royal.

"Deep and as blue as the seas he has sailed," replied Morgiana. She nodded at the pile of bags that had been taken from the carpet. "I think we should stop talking like all the other maids about the handsome Sinbad and start transporting our cargo to Sinbad's ship that lies yonder." She turned and caught the attention of the three boys who were hooked on every word between Sinbad and Baba. They reluctantly turned and headed to where Morgiana and Royal were standing, each holding two bags.

"Come on, guys," said Worm.

They all took the remaining bags, Worm, Chief and Shakers also picking up Baba's load to carry to Sinbad's ship.

The ship seemed to blend in with the surrounding green of the jungle; the canopy of palm leaves making the ship almost invisible from the sky. Then, again, how many magic flying carpets or giant birds carrying entire elephants would be looking for an old sailor and his boat? That is, if the rumors of a wealthy old sailor and his ship filled to the gunnels with treasure had spread far and wide and others, believing in rumors, were now looking for Sinbad the Sailor.

*****

Dinner that night was a welcome change for everyone. Morgiana and Baba were delighted to see their masquerade of being loyal servants to the evil Sultan coming to an end.

Sinbad welcomed his new guests and the opportunity to dine with friends and not being constantly on guard. His inner warning system still functioned while he ate, but now he had company to enjoy and enjoy he did. He was their chef for the evening preparing grilled fish he speared from the lagoon before the mouth of the camouflaged river. There was fresh fruit he quickly harvested from a wild orchard of trees that were foreign to Royal, Worm, Shakers and Chief. The fruit may have looked different from anything the four had ever seen, but it was the most delicious and they ate their fill.

"I'm stuffed," said Shakers.

"Me too," said Royal.

"Make that me three," said Worm.

Chef let out a belch. "Mister, Sinbad, sir," said Chief, "my people will make me the head of our tribe when I get back home and show them how to make fish like you did." He belched again, didn't excuse himself and continued to talk to Sinbad as if he had known him his entire life. "How long do you think it will take us to get back to Chicago from here?" he asked.

"That depends, my young friend," replied Sinbad. He paused

and looked off to the horizon where a bright golden glow had formed by the setting sun. "If we have favorable winds and hospitable seas, it shouldn't take too long." He smiled. "I don't think it will take us any longer than a year, year and a half at the most." He stared at Chief loving the look on the young man's face and then broke out into laughter. Baba and Morgiana joined him.

"What's so funny?" asked Chief.

"Yeah, Mister Sinbad the Sailor, sir," added Shakers. "I don't think we have enough survival stuff in those bags Baba made us carry out of the cave where we were at that will last a year. Maybe not even a month."

"Yes, sir, Mister Sinbad," said Worm, "I mean my grandfather gave each of us a wish and we could use those, I think, to get home safely."

Sinbad smiled and said, "provided you word the wish properly and don't squander them." He paused. "I believe you're down to just two wishes left, is that not so?"

"It is, sir," said Worm. "But, how did you know?" He noticed Baba smile.

"When you have lived through a thousand and one Arabian nights, Mister Worm," said Sinbad casually, "you have lived a life of learning. A Thousand and one Arabian Nights are filled with almost as much knowledge possessed by Allah, the holy one and all knowing. You already know that from reading about those Thousand Nights, do you not?"

Worm nodded. "But how long will it take us to get home, sir?" he added, his voice matching the look on his face.

Sinbad looked at Morgiana and Baba. "If I had these two as part of my crew, we would be in your Chicago in the blink of an eye."

"What do you mean if?" asked Worm.

Royal started to cry and reached for Morgiana's hand. "You're not coming?" she asked, her question choked. "But why?"

Both Morgiana and Baba acted as if they didn't understand why the four-young people were now very upset.

"Hey," said Chief. "I know I act like a big shot and shoot my mouth off, but we could've never gotten away from that lard butt Sultan and his gang of henchmen if it weren't for you two guys putting your necks on the line for us. We know that," he continued. "And, I know sure as God or your Allah made little green apples that we ain't getting back to Chicago without your help." Chief tried to look defiant and said, "So, there, Squares."

Sinbad, Baba and Morgiana looked at each other questioning.

Then Baba spoke. "Master Chief and you other three fine, brave, young people, our jobs, mine and Morgiana's are almost done. We have no choice but to go back to Baghdad and return to the streets and alleys from whence we came. Allah has willed it. This is our fate in life. We help others in need. We come to the aid of those who are going to be persecuted; those who are going to even be put to death by the evil that tries to rule the world. Morgiana's bravery saved a man named Ali Baba from certain death. Single handedly she systematically eliminated forty thieves who had terrorized and robbed both the rich and the poor storing their plunder in that cave that provided us with shelter and the goods to survive. You four-young people from that far away land called Chicago, have no idea how many times you came to be entering your heaven had it not been for the cunning and bravery of Morgiana."

Morgiana cleared her throat. "I believe I had assistance from you, Baba," she said, a slight smile forming. "And, don't forget that musty, dirty old carpet that you dug up from the city wall; that carpet that got us all out of the castle in one piece and save us from the army of the One Hundred and the Black Stallions." She nodded her head several times. "No small feat even with the help of Allah."

Sinbad began to clap his hands as if applauding, his applause almost a mockery. "Enough, my brave friends," he said. "Word travels fast in this part of the world where reality and the mysterious often collide. Today and tonight is a joyous time, a welcome repast for myself who has been destined to live alone. All of you have brought rays of sunshine into my life by your visit. You have also brought new challenges; new mountains to climb; more battles to fight and to rid the world of evil dressed as monsters and ghouls possessing no morals or scruples." He walked to Morgiana and Baba and put his arms around them both. "You have done well, my friends as I knew you would. The moment Allah gave me his sign of what was about to happen I was blest knowing that I would be in the company of two brave souls and once again work with you both."

"You knew Morgiana and Baba?" asked Worm.

Sinbad nodded.

"I didn't read about that in the book my grandfather gave me," he said.

Sinbad smiled.

"Wow," exclaimed Shakers.

"Oh, my, God," said Royal

Chief looked at Sinbad and Baba then smiled, finally saying: "Holy crap!"

*****

There were hugs and handshakes, even tears as the night wore on. It was Sinbad who did the hand clapping this time, getting the attention of the group. "We sail with the morning tide my friends," he stated sounding like the captain of a ship which he was. "We must stow this gear," he said pointing at the bags. "And, then, I must give my new crew of four a lesson in seamanship and how to survive on the briny when the wind doesn't blow and the ship doesn't go." His kind, smiling blue eyes looked at each of the six members. Two rows of white teeth sparkled from the glow of the vanishing embers that had cooked both their welcome and farewell feast. "I must also teach these four fine young people how to defend themselves from dangers out there," he said pointing at the darkness that blanketed the ocean. "Dangers that I hope we will not encounter, but, if we do, it is my duty to get them home to their loved ones safely regardless of how smelly their home may be."

Baba and Morgiana had helped carry the bags aboard Sinbad's ship. All of the bags went below deck without Sinbad giving an order. Gear under a deck would be protected from wind, waves and rain. That gear would be easily accessible when needed. So far, all Worm, Chief, Shakers and Royal knew about the gear was that it contained things to eat; things to make their journey home more enjoyable and safe. What they didn't know is that some of the bags possessed magic; powerful magic that would eventually help save their lives. Sinbad and the other two knew that. They had hoped and prayed magic wouldn't be necessary on this Sinbad's last voyage.

Before the four-young people realized, the sun was making an appearance in the eastern sky. They had a hasty meal of fruits and what tasted like store bought white bread. "It is time, my friends," said Sinbad to Morgiana and Baba. They understood and nodded. Turning, they started to leave the ship where they would go down the gang plank, climb aboard the magic carpet and head back to Baghdad and continue with their individual missions to help others in need.

"Don't go," said a sad Royal to Morgiana. "I don't even know you and I'm missing you with my whole heart and soul."

Morgiana smiled at her and gave her a hug. "I'm missing you too," she said, her kind eyes smiling.

"Come on, man," said Chief sounding his best defiant self, "Drag that old rug of yours on board and sail with us for awhile. You can fly back to land whenever you want."

"Yeah, stay," said Worm. He couldn't ever remember feeling so sad about seeing someone leave his life, perhaps forever. "You guys are the best."

"Wow," said Shakers surprising everyone by standing between Morgiana and Baba and putting his arms around their shoulders. "I know my late mom and dad would approve of you two being my new parents." He grinned at both of them, "Now, my Grandma River, she's a different story." His grin widened and then the corners of his mouth sagged. "Thank you for everything you did. I'll never forget you both." His arms slid from their shoulders and he walked to the other side of the ship where he stood staring off at the horizon. No one saw the tears streaming down his cheeks. Then, suddenly her turned and ran to them shouting: "Selfie!"

Royal, Chief and Worm dug into their pockets and pulled out their cell phones.

"I hope my battery isn't dead," said Worm.

"With all of that wedding stuff going on at the palace I totally forgot about this," said Royal holding up her phone.

"Me too," said Chief.

Shakers became the organizer and was leading a dumbfounded Morgiana, Baba and Sinbad down the ship's gang plank. "Stand right here, guys," he said excitedly while trying not to be too pushy. Before Morgiana, Baba and Sinbad realized, there were three rapid flashes almost blinding them.

"What by the beard of the prophets was that?" asked Baba rubbing at his eyes.

"Look," said Shakers unable to control his excitement. He almost pushed his phone up against Baba's nose.

Royal was subtler than her three male friends; almost apologetic and showing a touch of melancholy as she showed the group picture to Morgiana.

"Ah, so this is what you westerners refer to as a Selfie," she said. "I've only heard of these but have never seen one." She paused and smiled at Royal. "Princess, you look beautiful."

"No," replied Royal. "You're the one who is truly beautiful and I shall cherish this picture of you forever."

Both women hugged, Royal's eyes showing the start of tears.

"None of that, Princess," said Morgiana.

"Amen to that," said Sinbad. "Besides, no one who ever sailed on my ship cried." He gave a look of disapproval. "Sailors have enough salt water without adding more with tears."

There were bursts of laughter and a giggle or two. In that short time, none of the others saw Morgiana and Baba walk to the flying carpet and get on. Before the four musketeers could make a move or say a word, they heard Baba's hands clapping together.

"No," Royal managed to say as she saw the magic carpet lift

off the ground. Then she ignored Sinbad's remark about salt water and tears when she saw Morgiana smile at her and blow her a kiss.

Only Shakers had the alertness to have his cell phone camera at the ready. Flashed lit up the sky until the magic carpet was out of sight. "Gramma, you ain't ever gonna believe this," he muttered.

Chapter 11
Seamanship,
Sea Legs and Sea Sick

Sinbad's ship eased out of the crystal-clear stream and the shaded protection of the jungle canopy into bright, almost blinding golden morning. There was barely a chop on the water. Before Worm, Chief, Shakers and Royal could enjoy the scene and experience being on a sailing ship for the first time, Sinbad began directing them.

"You three able bodied seamen," he said to the three boys as he pointed, his finger indicating what he wanted them to do. "Grab 'hold of that line and pull when I give the command."

The three headed to the center of the vessel where a single, large mast stood, a series of ropes neatly tied.

"And, you, Miss Princess," he said to Royal. "Go aft and take the helm." He pointed at a long wooden arm like apparatus that protruded forward from the back of the ship.

Royal did what she was told, but only in part, standing alongside the ship's helm.

"This here vessel doesn't steer itself, Miss Princess," said Sinbad. "Grab hold and don't do anything until I give you the command."

Royal did what she was told, her slender arms being dwarfed by the size of the helm's handle.

"You three," said Sinbad aloud, "grab hold of that center line."

The boys barely had a chance to get a hand hold when they

heard Sinbad's command.

"Heave-ho!"

Not sure of what to do, they began pulling in earnest. They were surprised to see a long section of what looked like a dark canvass stretch out from a horizontal shaft that stuck out from the mast. They pulled harder and faster, the canvass creeping up the mast. Each grunted and strained under the weight as they continued to pull until the canvass reached the top of the mast and spread out in a gentle billow.

"Secure that line there," he said pointing to a series of wooden dowel like rods. "And, you, Miss Princess push the helm hard in that direction." His finger had tuned into a waving hand as he scurried to check on the secure line the boys had fastened, keeping his eyes on the sail filling out even more. Then he quickly joined Royal at the helm, making a slight adjustment. "Keep it steady as she goes," he said to her, the order now like more of a polite suggestion.

As quickly as he had appeared at the helm, he was now heading back to where the three boys were standing waiting. They didn't wait for long. "Follow me, mates," he said, sounding like the loving fathers they had left what seemed so long ago.

Sinbad led them to an opening in the deck that had been covered by, what looked to the three, a wooden door. "Last man in be sure that hatch is secure and follow me."

Each gave the hatch a quick glance and followed the captain who had disappeared under the deck. Worm was the last and he did what Sinbad had ordered. He pulled the hatch shut and made sure it was secure.

They found going down the ladder awkward at first. Getting used to the dark after being in the bright sun was even harder.

Sinbad had walked along a narrow corridor outlined by wooden supports that held up the sides of the ship. Stowed in between the supports were all of the bags they had brought with them from the magic carpet along with other crates, boxes and what appeared to be several large clay jars like the ones they had seen in the bazaar. "You," he said pointing at Chief, "take that jug top side." His finger quickly shifted to a jug. "And, don't drop it. Not if you want to go thirsty all the way to that place called Chicago."

Chief did what he was told.

"You take that bag there," he said to Shakers as he pointed at a pile of large, dark bags. "Bring that one on top up on deck and stow it in out of the sun. We don't want our food cooked just yet."

Shakers staggered under the weight of the bag that Sinbad helped put on his shoulder as if he were placing a pillow taken from Shakers' bed at home.

Worm watched Shakers struggle up the ladder, but not for long. "Ballast," he heard Sinbad say. "Do you know what that is?"

Worm remembered reading about ballast in one of the Howard Peace books and his still hero, Todd Moran. "Yes, sir," replied Worm respectfully.

"Good," said Sinbad pointing to a vacant area across from where they were standing. "Now start moving those wooden crates from where they're at over to that space over there. "We need to compensate for the winds that are going to come later today."

"Winds?" asked Worm politely. "The day is bright and calm."

"Did you ever hear of the saying, 'Red skies at night, sailors delight. Red sky in the morning, sailors take warning'?"

"No, sir," said Worm. He looked at Sinbad. "The sky was bright red this morning,"

"That it was, Mate."

They had the crates moved and tied down to the deck with long lengths of heavy rope that they found neatly coiled in a space next to where the crates would go. "Good job, Worm," said Sinbad. He paused then asked. "Why are you called, Worm?"

*****

The day continued on. Worm could see no notice of a storm as he looked in every direction. Royal still held on to the helm, not moving it one inch. Chief and Shakers helped Sinbad put together a lunch of fruit and bread.

"We need to eat the fresh food first," he said as he placed a folded cloth about three feet square on the deck. On the cloth was an assortment of bananas and melons. He peeled a banana and placed half of it in his mouth. "No time for manners and formality at sea," he said, his one cheek bulging out. "I'm going to relieve the Princess at the helm so she can eat." He got up and looked at the three. "When all of you are through eating I want you to clean up here and then I have a few easy jobs for you." He turned and headed in the direction of the helm.

The three continued to sit on the deck waiting for Royal to join them.

"Go join your friends and eat," Sinbad said to Royal as he placed his sun baked hands on the helm. "I'll' take over now."

"Thank you," said Royal as she released the rough wooden handle and hurried forward to join her friends sitting on the wooden deck. There was a discussion going on with Worm appearing to be the leader.

"Chief," said Worm. "When you used your wish to get away from those crazy guys and those demented horses why didn't you wish to be back home in Chicago? Heck, man, you could've been safe and away from all of this sailing stuff."

Chief looked at Worm very serious. "You know darn good and well why I used that wish of mine the way I did. All of you do."

Worm and the others looked questioningly at Chief.

"The code, dummies," replied Chief.

His friends looked at one another, their faces still questioning.

"Our oath. Our motto. You know, one for all and all for one," he said sounding frustrated. Then he broke into a grin. "Only this time I went first."

The others started laughing,

"Hey, guys, I couldn't have wished to go home without you. What kind of musketeer would I be?"

They waited for Royal to finish eating and pointed at what was left over on the cloth. "Well," said Worm as he stood up. "Sinbad gave us specific orders to clean up so we'd better get on the ball and do it."

Chief and Shakers looked at each other with Chief saying: "I ain't so sure I like the idea of throwing those food scraps over the side so the sharks can be our new best friends."

Royal looked at her three friends, the one word she had just heard etched across her shocked face.

SHARKS!

As Worm headed toward the hatch and what he had been told was the galley, he could see Royal walking back toward the helm and Sinbad. The wind had picked up and so did the size of the waves. From barely a white cap, the waves had almost triple in size and were now formidable, but not causing the ship to roll any more than usual. The bow dug easily into the waves and the ship continued to travel in what they could judge was a westerly course.

Worm had finished checking to see that all of the items in the ship's galley were securely put away and he quickly joined his friends at the stern of the ship where they were gathered near Sinbad.

"Now here are your orders for the rest of the day," announced Sinbad. He smiled at them. "I want you to walk along my ship and inspect it from stem to stern, port to starboard, gunwale to gunwale." He noticed their questioning looks. "Those are the sides of this here ship," he said with a grin. His head went from side to side. "You four landlubbers will learn soon enough," he said. His smiled disappeared. "Much sooner than you think," he said, his words sounding as if he were making a prophecy as his eyes scanned the horizon.

The four did what they were told. They made a game out of familiarizing themselves with the ship turning the tour into a television quiz show. As they grew weary with game playing and exploring, they decided to sit down on the deck in the bow of the ship. They enjoyed the warmth of the sun and the breeze. The motion of the bow going up and down relaxed them at first. They talked about what they would tell their parents when they got back home. None of the four said their parents would believe a word of what they would tell them.

"Flying carpets," said Chief. "I'd be run out of the tribe." He reached in the back pocket of his jeans and pulled out his cell phone. "I sure hope the pictures we took turn out."

"You ain't the only one," said Shakers as he saw Worm take out his cell phone. "Any signal?" he asked.

"Nah," answered Worm. "Just like when we were in the alley back in Baghdad."

"My Grandma River would slap me silly if I didn't have the pictures I took as evidence," said Shakers. "She'd tell me I would burn in Hell for lying." The group laughed.

"I don't need these pictures," said Worm. "My grandpa would believe me when I told him what happened," said Worm. "Remember, he was the guy that gave us those miniature scimitars and the wishes." He looked at his friends. "We only got two of those wishes left," he said reminding his friends. "I got mine and Shakers you got yours, right?"

Shakers nodded.

Before they realized, several things had happened. First, their conversations about cell phone pictures and Selfies had them checking their phones.

"Guys," said Shakers to the others. "I think we should somehow find a way to keep our phones dry just in case the weather turns nasty."

"The weather ain't gonna turn nasty," said Chief as he stood up and looked out over the bow. "I think Sinbad's just trying to scare us."

"He's doing a good job," said Shakers.

Worm's eyes traced the horizon. "I don't see no storm, but the wind is definitely blowing a lot harder than before."

The second thing that got their attention was the first shower of sea spray that had been kicked up by the wind. The cold sea water was like a wet slap in the face.

What really caught their attention was the increased motion

of the ship and the feelings in each of their stomachs that resembled the ship's unpredictable motion.

"I think we should head back to join Royal and Sinbad," said Shakers, his stomach beginning to send him messages that it wasn't liking the increased pitching and rolling of the ship.

They worked their way aft holding onto the ship's railing the way Sinbad had said earlier. They continued to talk but their eyes were not on each other. They were looking off to the horizon. They noticed that more and more clouds had moved in. As the clouds grew in size they also changed from a bright white to a grey. The winds had also increased. With the increase in the up and down motion in the bow was now joined by the bow banging into the waves. The banging was joined by the ship starting to roll from side to side more than it had earlier. As if on cue, they all sped up their pace as they continued to look back at Sinbad and Royal who were controlling the large helm. What they also noticed was that Sinbad had two hands on the helm. Royal was hanging on to it as if it meant her living or dying.

Sinbad had been right. A storm was approaching; a big and nasty storm.

The ship began to roll and pitch even more and the four found themselves falling to the deck as if they had never taken a step before. They soon discovered that they had to go to their hands and knees first to stand. Then they latched on to the side rail before standing up. They were surprised that they almost fell over from the bouncing and rolling of the ship. Continuing to hold on to the ship's railing with every ounce of strength they had, the four finally made their way to Sinbad. He didn't seem to notice them at first, his eyes glued to the skies that had now taken on a sickly black color.

"Looks like we're in for a bit of weather, Mates," said Sinbad to the four. "No need for concern, though," he said his voice full of reassurance. His voice did not match the look on his face. "This here ship has stood up too much more than this little zephyr of a breeze is going to give us."

The captain's words had no sooner left his lips when there was a loud crashing sound. Jagged streaks of lightning shot across the ominous, ugly clouds as if trying to shred them in a million pieces. His order was next; a short order of three words screamed into the howling wind, but not lost on his passengers: "Grab that line!" he yelled, his voice besting the wind and startling his crew of four. He pointed at the long thick rope that ran from the bow of the ship to the stern. "Grab it and hang on tight."

They followed Sinbad' order and just in time. As their arms intertwined through the rope and their hands latched on for dear life, a wave three times as high as the boat came crashing over the bow and washed over all of them. They all hung on to the rope except Sinbad. He clutched the long thick handle of the rudder steering the ship into the storm.

Wave after wave crashed over the bow; each one attacking the young crew members as if trying to claim them for the sea. Arms ached and hands burned, but the four hung on learning to put their heads down and suck in as much air as they could into their lungs. Experiencing the force of one wave was the only lesson they needed. Heads continued to go down and lungs sucked in air. Then mouths clamped shut, hands and arms squeezed tight on the thick, rough rope, feet tried to dig in to the wooden deck and legs braced for another round of bettering. Youthful muscles met Mother Nature's violence. Waves continued to pour over the bow of the boat. Talking was impossible. If one of them opened their mouth all that came out was sputtering punctuated with sea water. Then, as quickly as the storm had hit, it was gone, still heading in the same direction with a vengeance, but with no booty to lay claim for the sea.

"Good job, me mates," Sinbad yelled out as the wind returned to its normal bluster.

The four felt relieved, tired and thankful they were all safe. "Gather round me and sit," they heard Sinbad say as if nothing had happened.

"Time to catch your breath and dry out," he said indicating with the motion of his hands that they should form a semi-circle at his feet.

They did what they were told, sitting and looking up at their captain and their means to getting them back to Chicago. Trickles of doubt had begun to creep into their minds. Chicago was a long way off. How far off and how long to get there were questions none of the four had answers. What they knew was that they still had two wishes.

"That storm kind of reminded me of my very first voyage," Sinbad started out looking into each one's eyes; his own eyes seeming to sparkle with a faraway look. "Would you believe that it was a giant sleeping whale caused waves greater than what we faced today?"

The four looked up, silent, not questioning.

"Aye, mates," he continued his voice beginning to be interspersed with some drama. "The seas are filled with countless wonders; wonders the likes I have still to see and wonders that would fill your eyes with sights you would never believe." He let out a loud laugh. "Of course, if you had been with me when that giant sleeping behemoth woke up from his salty sleep and attacked us, capsizing our boat, then you would know what I'm trying to tell you." Sinbad paused and gaze out to see for a moment. "Ah, a beauty that boat was," he continued as he retold his tale. "The whale smashed it into pieces of wood small enough to start a fire." He made a face of disgust. "Did you know that I was one of the few survivors?" he asked without waiting for an answer. "I ended up on this beautiful island; a real paradise. That's what I thought at first," he said. "I was safe and I was alive and so were three or four others."

Four sets of eyes soaked up his words.

"I've been on many an island in my time and each one can be deceiving no matter how beautiful and intoxicating it may appear." His gaze went out to sea again. "That beauty lasted only until the sun set. My, what a beautiful sunset it was too; all gold and glowing with traces of whites and reds streaking across the sky." He stopped and looked into each of the pairs of eyes looking up at him; all seeming to be in a trance, but each brain alert, calculating and piecing together the words into logical conclusions.

"That night," he continued his voice subdued and the adventurous excitement gone, the jungle, the trees and under-growth came alive."

That statement caught the attention of the four listeners. They didn't have time to ask.

"No, my young friends, the jungle didn't' get up and walk around hunting and stalking us," he said, a long pause followed. "But, one of the survivors decided to check out a noise, a strange kind of noise, something not human, and he walked to the edge of the jungle from where we were standing on the beach deciding where we would sleep that night. We didn't have to decide long."

The listeners gave their undivided attention.

"As this curious survivor got within an arm's length of the edge of the jungle, the plants seemed to reach out like giant snakes striking from all directions. They grabbed him and pulled him into the jungle, into the plants themselves it seems. All we heard were awful screams. Those didn't last long. What followed was worse.

Listeners' eyes asked.

"It sounded like the sounds of a million hungry mouths eating."

Chief got to his knees. "Eating," he repeated. "Are you kidding us? Plants eating a human being?" he asked. "What did you and the others do?"

"The only thing we could," Sinbad answered calmly. "We were cautious. We had no idea what had happened because the night was black. We had no torches, no fire and no way to see. We called out the man's name over and over again, but we heard nothing. Not even the horrible sound of the eating and screaming. The jungle had turned quiet.

"That's all you did?" Chief asked.

"Until morning," answered Sinbad.

They all waited.

"At daylight, we armed ourselves with pieces of driftwood, parts of our ship, and carefully went to the edge of the jungle where our shipmate had entered. All we found were some traces of shredded clothing. There wasn't a sign of him. Not one single solitary sign. No blood. No nothing."

"Disappeared?" Chief muttered.

Sinbad nodded.

"How did you manage to get away?" asked Worm. "I mean, you said you were the only survivor."

"Yeah, man, what happened to the others?"

Shakers and Royal slid closer together, their near arms interlocking.

"When we found only the shredded clothing of our shipmate we decided to scour the beach for all the driftwood we could find."

"You built a raft," said Shakers his voice calm.

"Exactly," said Sinbad. "Very good, Master Shakers," he said. "Very good indeed."

Four facial expressions told him to continue.

"Are you sure?"

Four heads nodded, but not with enthusiasm.

"We built us a sturdy raft; one that we knew would get us over the coral reef that surrounded the island," he continued. "The tide had to be with us so that our raft wouldn't get crushed." Sinbad paused, seeming to be lost in thought. "What all of us didn't know about the treacherous jungle on the island is that it had scouts."

"Scouts," repeated Chief loudly, asking, questioning and wanting an explanation.

"I and the other discovered too late, too late for the others, that there were coiled vines at the edge of the jungle near the beach. The vines would slowly uncoil at night and go searching for food."

"You guys were that food, huh," said Chief more curious than scared.

Sinbad nodded. "The vines became like giant snakes. Anything that got near them they latched on to like a boa constrictor would crush its food before devouring it."

"How come you escaped?" continued Shakers.

"It was my time to guard the raft while the others slept. I was at the water's edge checking the knots we had fashioned out of some dead vines we found drifting along the beach. It was dark and I did the best I could while my mates slept about mid-beach just above the high tide line." His head went from side to side. "What we didn't know was that the high tide line was as far as those jungle scout vines went. Salt water was deadly to them. If my mates wouldn't have minded being awaken by a little sea water they would all be alive. I didn't see what happened mates. Again, it was dark. But, I saw shapes and forms, silhouettes I think you call them and I heard their agonizing cries. There was nothing I could do."

The four sat motionless continuing to listen, but their brains were anything but still.

Sinbad smiled at them and then continued. "I've had all kinds of adventures on my seven voyages," he continued. There were rivers filled with diamonds; giant birds that had eggs the size of boulders. I've escaped man eating monkey or gorilla like creatures."

"You mean like cannibals?" asked Worm beginning to feel uncomfortable; more from the stories than sitting on the wooden deck of their ship.

"Exactly," replied Sinbad. He smiled and continued saying: "Not to worry, my young friends. I don't anticipate any creatures with strange dietary habits in the direction we're heading. All of my other adventures were in the opposite direction of your Chicago. "he looked at the four and could see their apprehension. "It appears that it will be a beautiful night; one that is conducive to sleeping here on deck under the stars. Why don't you four go below and get your blanket and rugs and make sleeping spaces here on deck. It will be dark soon and movement then could be dangerous. I don't want to see any of you fall or be swept overboard."

They all looked at each other; the expression on their faces and in their eyes saying the one dreaded word: SHARKS!

*****

The four had arranged their bedding in a square forward near the bow of the ship where they could all see each other. Sinbad stayed by the rudder securing it with a stout line making sure it would steer the ship in a westerly direction.

The four whispered to one another so that Sinbad couldn't hear what they were saying.

"Sinbad sure has had quite the adventurous life," said Royal. "All of those voyages of his," she said sounding amazed. "How many did he say?"

"Seven," replied Shakers in a whisper.

"Seven too many for me," said Worm. "I prefer the adventures of Todd Moran myself."

"As far as I'm concerned," said Chief. "This voyage is one too many for me. I'm all for using one of our two wishes and getting home right now. That's right now as in pronto."

The other three glanced at Chief unsure of what to do. Then Worm said: "I think we should get a good night's sleep, think about this and talk about it in the morning."

"Worm's right," said Shakers. "Besides, we only have one wish left."

They stared at Shakers, faces questioning; eyes showing signs of fear.

Before any of them could say a word, Shakers said: "Why do you think that storm ended so fast?" He glanced at each of his friends. "Hey, guys, I'm not the best swimmer in the world and that's a big, big ocean out there. Sinbad is great and all that good stuff, but there's only one of him and there are four of us. And, besides, I don't relish the idea of swimming with no sharks."

The three looked at Shakers in disbelief.

"We have one wish left?" asked Royal.

"If I counted right," said Shakers. "But, you're the math whiz, Royal."

They all turned silent, minds cranking out scenarios; now, for the first time, they felt a sense of urgency. Chief was feeling panic.

"I say we use the last wish and we use it now," said Chief. "Worm, if I'm going to sleep on something, I want to sleep on it in my own bed back in Chicago. That's what I want," he continued being careful not to use the word, *wish*. "And, besides, who knows what other surprises Sinbad has in store for us? Heck, he's a nice guy and his stories are great. But, if those stories are anywhere near true, I don't want to meet no cannibals. I don't want to meet snakes large enough to eat elephants. I don't want to meet some monster from Jack and the Beanstalk. Forget it." He rolled over on his side and placed a forearm across his face.

Shakers propped his head up with his hand, his elbow being a brace. "I agree with Chief," he said softly. "No telling what we'll run into next. Like I said, this is a big, big ocean and we're on this little bitty boat. As great a sailor as Sinbad is supposed to be, he does get into a heap of trouble." Shakers closed his eyes and then they popped open. "And, did you guys notice, there are always a ton of dead people he leaves behind when he escapes safe and sound?"

"I noticed," said Worm.

"You're right," said Royal.

They all looked back to the stern where Sinbad stood, his muscular arms draped over the rudder even though a stout line had been fastened to it earlier. He appeared to be looking down at the deck. Had they looked more closely, they would have seen that he was asleep."

"Well," said Chief taking a quick look at each of his friends. "Are we, or aren't we?"

Shakers nodded.

"I do miss my parents," said Royal. "I know they're both wondering what happened to me." She gave a sympathetic look at Worm. "I hope your grandfather won't hate us."

"Hate who?" a booming voice asked. It was Sinbad.

They all jumped up as if they had been lifted up by a magical force.

"We don't hate anyone," said Shakers nervously. "Honest."

"Good," said Sinbad. "Hate is a terrible word."

"We know," replied Royal, her composure regained.

"Ah, Sinbad," said Chief. "We don't hate nobody. All we want is to get home safe and sound. And, that's without running into any of your old friends who wanted to end your life."

Sinbad's head went back and he let out a loud laugh. "Fear not, my friends, you'll be back home in that placed called Chicago before you know it."

Worm cleared his throat. "Excuse me Mister Sinbad," he said then clearing is throat again. "I'd like to," he said, then he paused. "We'd like to thank you for everything you've done for us. We really appreciate it. We really do. But, we're not so sure about what this stuff is about before we know what it really means." He took a deep breath. "Mister Sinbad, thank you. He paused. "Mister Sinbad, we have to say goodbye now."

Sinbad's eyes smiled and seemed to understand.

Worm continued. "Mister Sinbad we wish that we were back in Chicago.

Chapter 12
Sweet Home Chicago

They felt that the sea had erupted again into a drenching deluge. Heavy rain pelted them as blinding flashes of lightning seemed on a mission to make them glow in the dark. The winds howled around them as each of them grabbed at a metal rail, hands squeezing and legs once again braced.

"Darn it, Worm," Chief managed to shout over the wind. "I thought you said you were wishing that we were back home."

"I did," Worm shouted back.

"Yeah, Right," hollered Chief. "We're going to drown out here just like Shakers said."

"We ain't gonna drown, Chief," hollered Worm. "Look around."

A steam of light illuminated them and a large figure came into view.

"Oh, damn, it's Sinbad," muttered Chief.

It wasn't.

"Daddy," cried Royal.

*****

Before the four friends realized they were being helped off the front porch and into the safety of Royal's house by her father. Royal hugged her father who was soaking wet while the three guys stood like proverbial drowned rates, hair dripping and pools of water forming where they stood on the small welcome mat in the front entrance of the house.

Royal continued to hug her father and was about to try and explain what had happened, their meeting Baba and Morgiana, sailing home with Sinbad and the using of the four wishes that Will's grandfather had given them when her father gently pushed her away still holding her at an arm's distance.

"Don't you kids ever listen?" he asked, his question more of reprimand. "I told you before you went out that the weather was turning bad; that severe storms were forecast," he continued, his eyes stern, but his concern for his daughter's well being and the well being of the others showed through. "We're talking severe thunder and lightning; a possibility of a tornado."

Will didn't know why he said what he said next, but he got everyone's attention. "Sir," he started out addressing Royal's father. "I read where there are no tornadoes at sea. Instead they are called typhoons."

Three blank looks joined Royal's dad's jaw seeming to drop to his belt buckle. "What sea are you babbling about?" Royal's father asked. "Didn't that favorite teacher of yours at Thorpe ever tell you anything about that you live near one of the Great Lakes? You know, as in Lake Michigan."

"I'm sorry, Sir," Will said feeling and looking beyond embarrassed. "I guess I was thinking about a book I read once about this guy, he was a little older than me, who ran away from home and joined the merchant marines. He was in a lot of typhoons and stuff."

Royal's father let go of a huff and said, "You'll hear a lot more than stuff from your dad and your grandfather after I tell them what you four did." He pulled his daughter to him and gave her a hug. "Geez, going out in an electrical storm with tornado warnings," he said. "Do you four have a death wish?"

*****

The three boys were driven home by Royal's father after the storm had blown itself out over Lake Michigan. He made it a point to talk to each of their parents and taking extra time to calm down Shakers' grandmother who repeated Mr. Smolinski' comment about not listening, hers more demonstrative, the words accompanied by a damp dish towel whizzing by her grandson's head.

"Grandma," pleaded Shakers as he held up his cell phone. "Will you please stop with the towel and look at these pictures." He ducked.

*****

Chief's parents were appreciative of the ride their son got and thanked Mr. Smolinski; Chief's dad saying, "Can I give you a little shot of fire water to get you through the rest of your trip?"

"No thanks," Mr. Smolinski replied with a grin. "I'll take a rain check. Besides, I still have young Mister Sizemore to drop off."

Both men shook hands and Chief's dad nodded his head in the direction where he wanted his son to go. "Thanks again," he said to Mr. Smolinski.

Chief headed in the direction where his dad had nodded, the kitchen. He hoped there would be something to eat and not more lectures.

His mother had made him a BLT and poured him a giant glass of his favorite, chocolate milk. As he tore a chunk out of his sandwich, he saw his parents standing by the kitchen table. He knew what would follow.

"Well," his father said.

*****

Will's dad and grandparents were also appreciative of their son being driven home, the rain having picked up a second wind, but there were no fireworks provided by Mother Nature. His grandmother knew her son would be starving when he got home and had place a platter of cold cuts, assorted cheeses, lettuce, tomatoes and a container each of mustard and mayonnaise. There was also a glass of A & W root beer.

"Hey, Will," his father had said. "Do you want me to make you some lima beans?"

Will tried not to smile.

His grandfather laughed and then said, "When you finish eating maybe you can tell me what your friends thought of those fancy toothpicks."

Will reached in back pants pocket and removed his cell phone. He looked and almost died. The phone was covered with moisture from the storm. "Oh, no," he muttered. His finger gently pushed at the on button of his phone and he could hear his heart beat. It sounded like it was ready to explode. "Okay," he almost yelled when he saw the screen illuminate. "Grandpa, I think you're going to see all about your toothpicks." The first picture came into view and he grinned. "And, Grandpa, we didn't have to use your semaphore signal at all."

Chapter 13
Seeing is Believing

The Musketeers returned to school on Monday morning meeting at Mr. Toll's tiny Assistant Principal's office tucked away in the rear of the school near a loading entrance. They could hardly wait to tell him about their weekend and the four wish scimitars.

"Do you think he'll believe us?" asked Shakers as they neared the office door.

"I think he will," said Chief looking confidant. "He'll make fun of us like always, but he'll listen."

"I agree," said Royal as the group stopped in front of the Assistant Principal's open door. There were two other people in his office.

Will politely knocked on the door frame.

"Hey, Will," said Mister Toll in his jovial tone. "Just the man I want to see. Are the other Musketeers with you?"

"Yes, sir," answered Will stepping out of the way so his three friends could step into view. "One for all like always."

"Good," said Mister Toll twisting at the ends of his unruly mustache. "We have a new student who just moved in from New York. I'd like you to meet her and her mother."

"We'd like that," said Will.

"Did you say, her?" asked Royal stepping in front of the three guys and standing behind the two-people seated in front of Mr. Toll's desk. Royal froze in place. The older woman, the girl's mother, looked like Royal's mother's relative who had been rumored to be the queen of Iran. Royal could feel her knees turn to jelly as she looked at the new student. "Morgiana," she managed to say.

The girl turned, smiled and said, "How did you know my name was Morgiana?"

"Because I just met someone this weekend who looks exactly like you," stammered Royal as she tried desperately to keep calm.

"And what is your name?" asked the girl.

"Farah," replied Royal finding it hard to breathe.

Morgiana smiled at Royal and the others. My mother and I just moved here from New York. We had immigrated from Iraq. From Bagdad."

Before any of them could say a word, Mister Toll stood up and said: "The bell's about to ring. I want you four characters to show Morgiana around Thorpe and make sure she enjoys her time here. By the way, she'll be graduating with you this spring." He gave the Musketeers one of his famous warning looks. "Of course, I'm not so sure about whether three of you will be graduating." He glanced at Royal. "Of course, you will Farah. You'll be the valedictorian and graduate summa cum laude." He smiled at Will, Rickey and Robert. "If you three can get your acts together, you might graduate come lousy."

Then Shakers startled all of them by asking: "Mister Toll, are your relatives from Baghdad?"

"Baghdad?" repeated Mister Toll. "Why do you ask."

"Because I met someone, we all met someone, this weekend who resembles you. His name was Baba."

"Sorry, Robert, but there are no Baba's in my family and none that I know of in our homeland of the Carpathian Mountains."

"Carpathians," repeated Ricky. "What in the heck are those?"

"What was that I said about you graduating come lousy?"

When the bell rang for the start of the day, Mister Toll gave the Musketeers a pass and assured Morgiana's mother that her daughter would be in good hands. As they all walked along the crowded hallway, Shakers said to Worm, "Did you ever hear of five Musketeers?"

Epilogue

Will's grandfather heard the front door open. He looked at his watch and wasn't surprised to see his grandson enter the living room. What made him to a double take was that Will was with his three friends who he had nicknames the Thieves.

His grandfather blinked and was unable to his amazement. There was a new face joining the group; a pretty, female face. "Welcome," said Will's grandfather. "And you are?"

The girl tried not to blush as she stayed polite, almost shy. "My name is Morgiana," she said, a slight accent in her voice.

Will's grandfather pursed his lips, the lines on his forehead seeming to get deeper. He repeated the girl's name and then said: "The only Morgiana I ever heard of was a female character in the story of Ali Baba and the Forty Thieves."

Morgiana's head did a slight bow and she kept her head downcast. Before any other words could be said, Will interrupted.

"Grandpa," said Will starting out as if he were walking on a living room floor covered with dozens of eggs, the shells all marked, Fragile.

Will's grandfather nodded at him.

"Well, Grandpa," continued Will sounding and appearing as if he were searching for the right words. "Grandpa," he continued, "Me and the others, well, we'd kind of like to know how you came about those tiny scimitars you gave us,"

His grandfather smiled and suppressed a chuckle. "Do you now," he said.

Five heads went slowly up and down.

"A long story," his grandfather said. "A boring story."

"That's okay, Grandpa," said Will. His statement was repeated in a mumbled way by the others.

"Those scimitars and their magic came from the original Disneyland."

Five pairs of eyes grew a little larger.

"I bought them there at a souvenir stand," he said, then pausing. "As a matter fact, I bought five of them." He stopped to recollect. "The lady who sold them to me said they were magic."

The five pairs of eyes asked the question even though they knew what the answer would be.

"That was a long time ago," Will's grandfather continued. "It was the first year Disneyland opened in California."

"You mean Florida and Disney World isn't the only park around?" asked Chief.

"You are correct, Sir," said Will's grandfather. I was just out of the Navy then and getting ready to come back home to Chicago. I was visiting with one of my buddies and his parents. He had also gotten discharged at the same time. We were close friends and we vowed to stay in touch." A laugh escaped the old man's throat. "We never heard from one another again."

"Really?" asked more than the eyes.

"Anyway, this lady who sold those scimitars to me said they possessed magic," he continued. "I didn't believe her for a second, but they looked cool so I bought them."

"Grandpa," asked Will politely. "When did you find out they were magical?"

Will's grandfather smiled. "When I made a wish," he said.

"You wanted to try them out?" asked Will.

His grandfather gave a nod.

"Why, Sir?" asked Shakers, an eagerness in his voice.

"Well, Robert," Will's grandfather said. "I found myself in a tough spot. My buddy had driven me to the airport. We had some car trouble and I was going to miss my flight. I told my buddy I would hitchhike to the airport and that he should stay with his car until a tow truck to get there. I was dressed in my uniform and was carrying my big sea bag. As I recall, I wasn't on the highway for a few minutes when I big old VW van pulled up. It was one of those that was painted with flowers and peace signs, all in loud colors. A girl on the passenger side asked me where I was headed and if I wanted a ride. I was most appreciative and I thanked them for their kindness. It didn't take me long to discover that those young people my age weren't being very polite."

"Why was that, Mister Sizemore?" asked Farah.

Will's grandfather gave a slight clearing of his throat. "Well, Farah, there was an unpopular war going on in Asia and there were quite a few people in this country protesting that war. Some of those protestors had even labeled anyone in uniform as baby killers, murderers and criminals."

"And that's what they thought you were?" asked Farah.

"I guess," Wills' grandfather continued. "Anyway, I knew I was in trouble when the van pulled off the main highway and ended up on side road. "Before I knew it, I was being thrown out of the van along with my sea bag and a couple of the guys got out as well. One I remember to this day. He was as big as a house and bald. He also pulled out what turned out to be a real, full-size scimitar."

Will's grandfather looked at the expressions on the faces of his audience. "You're not questioning the truth to my story?"

Five heads went slowly from side to side.

"Anyway, the only thing I could think of at the time were those miniature scimitars I carried in the pocket of my dress blues. I reached in and pulled one out and the big, bald guy started laughing at me."

"Wanna dual, sailor boy?" he asked sarcastically while swinging his own real scimitar in wide circles. Then the circles got real close and the look on the big, bald guy's face changed into something that resembled he meant business and that I was in big trouble; big trouble meaning I was going to be minus my head."

"I think I know what you did," said a very polite Morgiana.

"I made a wish," said Will's grandfather.

"Wow, Grandpa," said Will.

"Wow is right, William. Wow is definitely right."

Chief folded his arms across his chest. "You made a wish, saved your life and, then, years later you gave those little swords to Will and to us?"

"That I did."

"Grandpa," said Will. "Are you saying that Mickey Mouse saved us?"

Will's grandfather gave a shrug. "Mickey, Walt, Daisey Duck," he said. "Take your pick. You're here, aren't you? And with your new friend."

Title: Where Have All the Go-Go's Gone?

Part I

- Author: Richard Baran
- Publisher: TotalRecall Publications, Inc.
- Paperback, ISBN: 9781590952405
- Ebook, Nook, Kindle, ISBN: 9781590952412
- Number of pages: 304
- Publication Date: 2015

Bo Pepperwall's intelligence dwarfed Mensa's parameters. He was perceived as strange thereby resulting in his being ridiculed by many, shunned by most and being called, Bo the Schmoe by all. Then he faced a dilemma. He had to choose between money (which he never had) and morals (which he also lacked). Should he weasel a part of his recently widowed sister's inheritance for a business venture or should he turn in the killer of her husband, his despicable brother-in-law? He chooses both. Bo opens La Tinkerbelle's a Go-Go, a 1960's retro discotheque in an abandoned factory building in a Chicago slum using a theme from the legend of Peter Pan. Surrounding himself with bizarre employees (each having a unique vision of reality) who put fun into dysfunctional, his dream nearly goes bust. Then a Chicago gossip columnist prints a story that has customers lined up and Bo collides with his dilemma. The collision buries him in money and public adulation. Success, however, can't cover his moral guilt in the surprise ending to this murder mystery farce that is more farce than mystery.

Title: When Will They Ever Learn?

Part II Where Have All the Go-Go's Gone?

- Author: Richard Baran
- Publisher: TotalRecall Publications, Inc.
- Paperback, ISBN: 9781590952436
- Ebook, Nook, Kindle, ISBN: 9781590952443
- Number of pages: 220
- Publication Date: 2015

Bo Pepperwall, a card carrying member of Mensa, dreamer, conniver and ridiculed lifelong loser opens *La Tinkerbelle's a Go-Go*. A 1960's retro discotheque located in a Chicago slum, he uses a theme from the legend of Peter Pan that includes a scantily clad Tinker Bell. He finances his business by weaseling part of his sister's inheritance away from her. He also witnesses the murder of his despicable brother-in-law, the mayor of Glen Forest on the Watercourse, a prestigious Chicago North Shore community. Bo, however, remains a loser and his garish disco faces bankruptcy until an article by a Chicago gossip columnist turns it into a bonanza.   That same day, Tinker Bell's outraged mother accidentally sets fire to La Tinkerbelle's and destroys the booming business. Bo and his employees—along with two black cats named Heckle and Jeckle—end up in court charged with violations of the Mann Act; contributing to the delinquency of minors; ignoring EPA laws; cruelty to animals and presenting lewd and indecent performances. Bo turns in the killer and the court finds him innocent of the criminal charges in the surprise ending to this murder mystery zany comedy.

Title: The Jacket

- Author: Richard Baran
- Publisher: TotalRecall Publications, Inc.
- Hard Cover ISBN: 9781590955659
- Paperback, ISBN: 9781590955666
- Ebook, Nook, Kindle, ISBN: 9781590955673
- Number of pages: 352
- Publication Date: 2013

Tidge Mackiewicz, new patriarch of his family, received several orders from his dying father, Kid Scream. One order stated that Tidge should quit believing in Santa Claus and stop acting like every day was Christmas. Tidge should also abandon his belief that the Luftwaffe shot down Santa Claus on Christmas Eve in 1944 and Santa survived.

Title: The Dutchman's Gift

- Author: Richard Baran
- Publisher: TotalRecall Publications, Inc.
- Paperback, ISBN: 9781590952979
- Ebook, Nook, Kindle, ISBN: 9781590952986
- Number of pages: 124
- Publication Date: 2015

A twelve year old boy finds a magical Apache arrowhead while hiking with his grandfather in the Superstition Mountains of Arizona. The arrowhead transports the boy from a Disney World rollercoaster ride back over one hundred and fifty years to the Superstitions where he meets "The Lost Dutchman."

Title: **Shutter Bug**

- Author: Richard Baran
- Publisher: TotalRecall Publications, Inc.
- Paperback, ISBN: 9781590953167
- Ebook, Nook, Kindle, ISBN: 9781590953174
- Number of pages: 176
- Publication Date: 2016

Emma Grace Waveland, a self-proclaimed Shutter Bug at twelve, finds herself transported from a safari in Disney World to Africa's Serengeti where she joins a group of professional hunters who capture wild animals for zoos. Her new adventure brings her face-to-face with deadly crocodiles, a giant rhino, a python, a lady photographer who looks like a young version of her great grandmother, hunters who resemble old movie stars and a camp cook with mysterious powers. Her family doesn't believe her when she returns from her trip, but she has evidence on her cameras' memory cards and her iPhone.

Title: Heroes and Idles

- Author: Richard Baran
- Publisher: TotalRecall Publications, Inc.
- Paperback, ISBN:
- Ebook, Nook, Kindle, ISBN:
- Number of pages: 186
- Publication Date: 2016

A burlesque star, Indian Chief, two cantankerous grandfathers, an Italian grandmother who drinks whiskey from a Mason jar, a Prussian officer and a Chicago Cub baseball star impact four young lives.

Tess, Stan, Georgie and Gil had their idols. Tess worshipped her World War II era burlesque star, Aunt Rose and an Ojibwa Indian Chief, John Proud Bear in *Lunch with a Gypsy*. Georgie, a young father entangled in an affair, drew guidance from his immigrant Italian grandmother, Nana Beam's whiskey induced lessons about repentance in *I've Got a Secret*. Stan idolized his two cantankerous grandfathers and their lesson he learned about the real world. It was the death of his wife and then his mother that led him back to his high school sweetheart from four decades ago in *The One that Got Away*. Thirteen year old Gil had three heroes. His Poppy Paul taught him to respect his given name, Gilead. Gil's father formally introduced him to Wrigley Field the day after the Chicago Cubs traded Gil's third idol, Andy Pafko to the Brooklyn Dodgers. Tragically, death claimed Gil's father soon after and Gil later found a unique way to keep his dad's memory alive in *Trading Prushka*.

Author Richard Baran

Richard Baran holds a doctorate and two masters' degrees besides his bachelor's in business. A Navy veteran, he taught and coached for forty years at the secondary school and collegiate levels. His first novel and award winning, *The Jacket* was published by Total Recall Press in 2014. Subsequent novels, *Where Have all the Go-Go's Gone? Book 1; Wehn Will They Ever Learn? (Where Have all the Go-Go's Gone?) Book 2, The Dutchman's Gift, Shutter Bug* and *Heroes and Idols* were published by TotalRecall Publications Other publishing credits include, *Coaching Football's Polypotent Offense*, a coaching text, a short story, *That Ain't No Walleye* and several dozen articles in professional business, education and coaching journals. He and his grammar school sweetheart, Carol Ann have eighteen grandchildren and they divide their year between Franklin Park, Illinois; Phoenix, Arizona, and Minocqua, Wisconsin.

Visit www.richardbaran.com for more information.

**A Mouse Gate Adventure Book
What's your adventure?**

www.mousegate.com